chapter one

SIERRA JENSEN GAZED OUT THE TRAIN window at the cold, wet English countryside. In an hour she and her friends would be back at Carnforth Hall with the other ministry teams that had spent the past week in various European countries. She wedged her hands between her crossed legs, trying to warm them against her jeans. Endless pastures, frosted with winter's ice, flashed past her window. Sierra let out a sigh.

"What are you thinking?" Katie asked, uncurling from her comfy position on the train seat next to Sierra. Katie's red hair swished as she tilted her head to make eye contact with Sierra. Even though Katie was two years older than Sierra and they had met only two weeks ago, they had become close during the week they had just spent together in Belfast, Northern Ireland.

"About going back to the States," Sierra said. Her silver, dangling earrings chimed as she turned to Katie. Sierra smiled her wide, easy smile at Katie, but she was really looking past Katie. In the seat across the aisle from them, their team leader, Doug, was sitting next to his girlfriend, Tracy.

"This whole trip went too fast," Katie said, folding her arms and settling back against the upholstered seat. "I'm not ready to go home yet."

"I know," Sierra agreed. "Me neither." She noticed that Doug was now slipping his arm across the back of the seat. Tracy slid closer to him.

"I'd like to come back," Katie said. "Maybe next summer."

"Me too," Sierra said, watching Tracy snuggle up to Doug.

"It would be great if our whole team could be together again for another trip."

"Me too," Sierra said. Tracy was tilting her heart-shaped face toward Doug's, giving him a delicate smile that, by the look on his face, melted him to the core.

"What do you mean, 'me too'? Of course you would be on the team." Katie looked over her shoulder to see what had distracted Sierra. Turning back to Sierra, Katie leaned forward and quietly said, "Don't they just make you sick?"

"Katie," Sierra said in a hushed voice, "I thought you guys were all best friends and had been for years, you, Doug, Tracy, and Christy. Why would it make you sick to see those two together?"

"We are all best friends. It's just . . . well, look at them! They're totally in love."

"I know," Sierra said, casting another quick glance at

Only You, Sierra

ROBIN JONES GUNN

BETHANY HOUSE PUBLISHERS
MINNEAPOLIS, MINNESOTA 55438

Only You, Sierra
Copyright © 1995
Robin Jones Gunn

Edited by Janet Kobobel Grant
Cover design by Praco, Ltd.
Cover illustration by Ed Little

Scripture quotations taken from the *King James Version of the Bible*, or from the *New King James Version of the Bible*, copyright © 1979, 1980, 1982, by Thomas Nelson, Inc., Publishers. Used by permission. All rights reserved.

Published by Bethany House Publishers
A Ministry of Bethany Fellowship International
11300 Hampshire Avenue South, Minneapolis, Minnesota 55438

Printed in the United States of America by
Bethany Press International, Minneapolis, Minnesota 55438

Library of Congress Cataloging-in-Publication Data

Gunn, Robin Jones, 1955–
    Only you, Sierra / Robin Jones Gunn.
       p. cm. — (The Sierra Jensen series ; #1)
    Summary: Normally a confident and adventurous sixteen-year-old, Sierra returns from a missionary tour in England to a number of unsettling changes in her home and family.
    ISBN 1–56179–370–1
    [1. Christian life—Fiction. 2. Moving, Household—Fiction. 3. Family life—Fiction. 4. Schools—Fiction.] I. Title.
II. Series: Gunn, Robin Jones, 1955–   Sierra Jensen series ; #1.
PZ7.G972On 1995   95–5722
                                                                        CIP
                                                                        AC

---

98   99   00   01   02   03   /   13   12   11   10   9   8   7   6

To some of my writer friends,
who hang out on the young adult
fiction shelf with me:

Lissa Halls Johnson, whose books
inspired me more than
a decade ago to write for teens;

Lee Roddy, who took the time to read
my poems when I was nineteen;

Marian Flandrick Bray,
ever the gracious hostess;

and Bill Myers, who, by his life,
will never let me forget
why we're writing.

The Lord our God in the midst
of thee is mighty!

the couple who were now talking softly and looking deeply into each other's eyes. "I can't imagine ever being in Tracy's place and having a guy look at me like that."

"Are you kidding?" Katie pulled back and let her bright green eyes do a quick head-to-toe scan of Sierra. "Have you ever looked in a mirror, girl? First, you have the hair going for you. You have great hair! Wild, blond, curly. Very exotic."

"Haven't you noticed?" Sierra said, tugging at a curly loop of her long hair. "Straight, sleek hair happens to be in right now."

"Oh, sure, this week. Wait a few days. Everyone will be running out for perms so they can look just like you. And your smile happens to be award-winning, in case you didn't know. Blue-gray eyes that change with the weather are also quite popular. A few freckles. That's good. Fantastic clothes, all very original. And I don't ever want to hear you complain about your body."

"What body? I'm shaped like a tomboy."

"Better to be shaped like a tomboy than a fullback."

"You're not shaped like a fullback," Sierra protested.

"Okay, a halfback."

"You're both beautiful," Stephen, the German guy on their team, inserted into the conversation. He was sitting directly across from them and had appeared to be sleeping.

Sierra felt her cheeks blush, realizing Stephen had overheard their conversation. He was the oldest one of their group, and his beard added to his older appearance.

"Why do women find it a sport to criticize themselves to their friends?" Stephen asked, leaning forward and taking on the tone of a counselor. "You both are gorgeous young women on the outside and fantastically beautiful here," he patted his heart, "where it really counts."

"Then you tell us why all the guys aren't falling at our feet," Katie challenged.

"Is that what you want?" Stephen, in an uncharacteristic move, tumbled to the floor and bowed at their feet.

Sierra burst out laughing.

"Get out of here!" Katie said. "You're making this a joke, and I'm serious."

Stephen returned to his seat, a satisfied little grin across his usually serious face.

"You're a guy; tell us what you're attracted to in a girl," Katie said.

Stephen took a quick look at Tracy and then back at Sierra and Katie. "Well," he began, but it was too late. His unspoken message seemed clear.

Katie threw up her hands in the air. "I knew it! You don't have to say anything. You men are all alike! You all *say* it's the personality and what's on the inside that counts. But the truth is your first choice every time is the Tracy-type, the sweet, helpful, cute ones. Admit it! There's little hope in this world for the few individualists like Sierra and me."

"On the contrary. You are both very attractive. To the right man, you will be a treasure. You just need to wait on God."

"I know, I know," Katie said. "And until then, we have our own little club, don't we, Sierra?"

Sierra remembered when she and Katie had formed the Pals Only Club at the beginning of their trip. She slapped Katie a high five and said, "P.O. forever!"

"That's right," Katie said. "We may have lost Tracy, but it's you, me, and Christy from here on out."

"You women do not need a little club," Stephen said. "Perhaps a caveman with a big club might be helpful . . ."

Instead of laughing at his joke, the girls gave Stephen a tandem groan and twisted their expressions into unappreciative scowls. He folded his arms across his chest, closed his eyes, and pretended to go back to sleep. But a crooked grin was on his lips.

"Come on," Katie said. "Let's get something to drink."

Sierra followed her down the rocking aisle that led to the back of the train car. They passed through the sliding doors and headed for the compact snack bar at the end of the next car. After buying Cokes, they stood to the side by the closed windows.

"Guys like Stephen really bug me," Katie said. "First they're all sweet and full of compliments, and then they make stupid jokes. You never know if they're serious about all the nice stuff or not."

"I think he meant it," Sierra said, shifting her weight from one foot to the other. She was wearing her favorite old cowboy boots that she had worn for most of the trip. They were actually her dad's old leather boots. Very authentic. She had found them in the garage last summer when they were cleaning out stuff for a garage sale. Her mom had wanted to sell them and said, "I can't believe we still have these old boots! Howard wore them on our first date."

That's when Sierra knew they couldn't be cast off to some stranger at a garage sale. She tried them on, and to her amazement, they fit. She had worn them constantly ever since, much to her mother's dismay.

"Enough talk about guys," Katie said. "Let's talk about something else."

"It'll be great to see all the other teams tonight and hear about everything that happened to them."

"Yeah," Katie agreed. "I can't wait to hear about Christy's week in Spain."

"I still can't believe they pulled her off our team at the last minute and sent her all the way to Spain after the rest of the Spanish team had already left. I don't think I could have done what she did, traveling all by herself for two days and then joining up with a team of people she barely knew."

"It's like I kept saying," Katie said, making a muscle man pose, "she is Missionary Woman."

Sierra smiled. "I felt as if I was just getting close to her, and then they shipped her off on a moment's notice. It must have been even harder for you to see her leave like that, since you guys have been best friends for so long."

"I'm sure it was a God-thing," Katie said, finishing her drink and tossing her can into the bin marked "rubbish" as if she were shooting a basketball into a hoop.

She made the shot and with two fingers gave herself a score of "two points" in the air.

Sierra finished her Coke and aimed her can at the rubbish bin. Her shot banked off the side. When she scooped it up, Katie said, "Try it again." Sierra did. This time she made it.

"All right!" Katie said, slapping a low five behind her back. "We're unstoppable."

Sierra thought of how much had happened during their week of ministry at the church in Belfast. Sierra and Katie had worked with the children, had performed in a drama group, had gone out street witnessing, had prayed with teenagers when they said they wanted to give their lives to God, and had visited some elderly women of the church who treated them to tea and cakes. It had been a life-changing experience for Sierra, and she was glad Katie had buddied up with her.

"You know," Katie said, as they headed back to their seats, "I'm sure God had a reason for taking Christy off our team. If nothing else, it let me get to know you, and I'm really glad for that."

"I am too," said Sierra. "I'm just starting to feel depressed now that it's almost over."

"Not so fast! We have two more days before we have to leave," Katie pointed out.

"Next stop is ours," Stephen said when they reached their seats. "Hey, Doug, we're almost there. Next stop."

Sierra watched as Tracy uncurled herself from Doug's shoulder and Doug resumed his role as team leader.

He was a great guy. Sierra admired him, especially after all they had experienced together as a team this past week. She could easily see Doug and Tracy married and working together in ministry.

The group members gathered their belongings, as they had done dozens of times during their travels, and helped with each other's luggage. It was a familiar routine.

Sierra fought off the sadness that crept in when she realized the next time she boarded a train in England it would be to go home. Something caught in her throat every time she thought about returning to the States. She hadn't been able to talk about it to Katie or anyone else. Maybe she should. Whenever she had mentioned her situation, it had been with her usual cheerful, adventuresome spirit. No one knew that deep down she was nervous, knowing that everything in her life was going to be different when she returned home.

While Sierra was in England, her family had moved. Instead of flying back to the small mountain community in northern California where she had spent her life, she was flying into Portland, Oregon, her new home.

The train came to a stop, and the group shuffled off and made its way through the station and then out to the small parking lot in front. A van was waiting for them in the late afternoon drizzle. They climbed in like a bunch of robots, all so accustomed to travel and so tired from their latest adventure.

Sierra sat in the back next to the window, curling and uncurling her cold toes inside the leather cowboy boots. She still had two more days in England, two more days to think through all the changes that were about to take place in her life. She wasn't ready for any of it. The nervousness about the move bothered her. Sierra had always been the bold, free-spirited type. But then, her whole foundation of home and family had never been rocked before.

Tracy slid into the van and plopped down next to Sierra. Doug sat in the front and patted the driver on the shoulder, thanking him for the ride.

Tracy said, "I can't wait to see Christy! I hope she had a good time in Spain."

Sierra smiled and nodded her agreement. She couldn't help but like Tracy. Everyone did. And of course Sierra was happy for Tracy that she and Doug had gotten together on this trip. Still, something made Sierra feel a little hurt and left out. Maybe it was jealousy, jealousy over Tracy getting one of the few truly wonderful guys left in the world.

The van wound around the narrow streets through the small town and then hit the country road leading to Carnforth Hall. The scenery looked exactly as it had a week ago when they left, with the exception of a few wild, purple crocuses popping up through patches of thawed earth. Sierra decided that if any more guys like Doug existed in this world, they certainly weren't in Pineville, Sierra's old hometown. And they certainly weren't on this trip.

"Tracy, by any chance does Doug have any brothers?"

"Does Doug have any brothers?" Tracy repeated with a skeptical look. "Why do you ask?"

"Oh, no reason. Never mind."

The van stopped in the gravel driveway at the front of an old castle, Carnforth Hall. Standing in front of the huge wooden doors was a tall brunette under an open umbrella. She waved wildly at their van.

"It's Christy!" Katie shouted, standing up in the back of the van and pounding on the closed window. "Hey, Missionary Woman!"

Sierra watched as Christy struck a muscle-bound pose with her right arm. Something on her wrist caught the glow of the amber porch light and sparkled brightly.

chapter two

KATIE LURCHED ACROSS THE VAN SEAT and grabbed Tracy by the shoulder. "Tracy, look!" she yelled. "On her wrist! Is that . . . ?"

"How could it be?" Tracy asked.

"Open the door, you guys!" Katie screamed.

Sierra couldn't figure out why Katie had gone berserk. Katie, who was the first one out of the van, grabbed Christy's wrist, looked at it, looked at Christy, and then screamed.

Tracy sprang from her seat and said, "Doug, it is!"

"It is what?" Sierra asked. "What's going on here?"

Doug was already out the van's front door and was joining Katie and Tracy in giving Christy a group hug. Then Doug asked Christy something and took off running in the rain without a jacket or umbrella to the administration offices.

"Do you have any idea what's happening?" Sierra asked Stephen.

"They're Americans," he said. "This is normal behavior for them, isn't it?"

"Hey, I'm an American, and you don't see me freaking out here, do you?"

"Not yet."

"Come on," Sierra said. "Let's find out what it is." They climbed out of the van into the steady drizzle and tried to break into the wild chattering between Tracy, Katie, and Christy.

Katie kept saying, "I don't believe it. I don't believe it. This is like the ultimate God-thing of the universe! I don't believe it."

"Sierra," Christy called out over Tracy's head, "hi."

The two girls hugged, and Sierra said, "Well? So what is this 'God-thing of the universe'?"

Christy held out her right arm and showed Sierra her wrist. She wore a beautiful gold I.D. bracelet. Sierra touched it and saw that it had the word "forever" engraved across the top.

"It's nice," Sierra said. "Did you get it in Spain?"

"Sort of," Christy said. "I mean yes, but . . . well, it's a long story."

"I just don't believe this," Katie said. She looked as if she needed to sit down.

"I'm so happy for you!" Tracy said, grasping Christy's arm and squeezing it.

"Pardon us if it seems rude," Stephen said, pulling his coat collar up around his neck. "But it does happen to be raining. We're going inside."

"Come on," Christy said, holding her umbrella high enough to cover as many gathered around her as possible.

"We probably should all go inside. I'll explain everything, Sierra."

The group members gathered their wet luggage and trudged through the gravel into the castle. The guys headed to their rooms, apparently not interested in Christy's secret. The four girls shook out their coats and hung them on the entryway pegs before heading for the great drawing room. A fire roared in the stone fireplace, but the couches around the fireplace were empty. Katie was the first to plop down.

"I still can't believe this," she said.

Sierra sat next to her while Christy and Tracy sat across from them. Sierra noticed that Christy looked different. Two weeks ago, when they had first met at Carnforth Hall, Christy had walked around every day with worry lines across her forehead and with a clenched jaw. Now she was radiant. Her eyes danced with the light from the fire, her cheeks looked warmed and pink, and her smile was contagious.

"I'm dying to hear what's going on!" Sierra said. "You look like a different person, Christy. Please don't tell me it's because you're in love or anything."

"Sierra," Christy said, trying to make a straight face, "I am so totally in love it even makes me sick!"

Tracy giggled joyfully. Katie slumped down in the couch and moaned. "I can't believe this is happening! Our club is dwindling, Sierra. It's just you and me now."

"I don't understand," Sierra said. "Can you really be

this in love with someone from Spain? Someone you met a week ago?"

"No, I mean yes. I mean, we didn't just meet," Christy fumbled. "Do you remember that night in our room when Katie told you about Todd?"

"Wasn't he the gorgeous blond surfer who went to be a missionary on some island?" Sierra asked.

Just then Doug's voice behind them said, "Well, you got three out of four right. He didn't go to any island."

Katie sprang from the couch and gave the guy next to Doug a long hug while she cried, "I can't believe this!" Tracy was right behind her giving the guy an equally long hug and shedding just as many tears.

Sierra felt as if she didn't quite belong since she didn't understand what was happening. When Christy rose to give Doug a sideways hug, Sierra stood up, walked around the couch to where everyone was hugging, and stood there grinning and feeling like a dork. Why was this reunion such an emotional one for all her new friends? Who was this Todd guy anyhow? What was the big deal about his being there and Christy being in love with him?

Tracy let go of Todd, and he looked over at Sierra. She met his gaze and caught her breath. Sierra was looking into the most incredible blue eyes she had ever seen. It was more than his eyes, though. There was a look about Todd. She could tell he was different from other guys. God was going to do something special through this man.

"Sierra," Christy said, "I'd like you to meet Todd."

Todd stuck out his right hand and shook Sierra's. He gave her a broad smile, which showed off the dimple on his right cheek. "Christy's told me a lot about you," Todd said. "I'm really glad to meet you."

"And from what we overheard," Doug added, "Christy has told you all about Todd."

Sierra felt a little embarrassed that Todd and Doug had heard her call Todd gorgeous. She also had a fleeting thought that if Doug didn't have a brother, maybe Todd did.

"We all thought Todd had gone to Papua New Guinea," Tracy said. "None of us has seen him for almost a year."

"But he was in Spain!" Christy said triumphantly. "He met me at the train station." Tears beaded up in Christy's eyes. She looked up at Todd and smiled. "With a big bouquet and my bracelet."

"Don't tell me," Katie said. "White carnations. Am I right?"

"Yeah," Todd said. "And do you know how long it took me to find white carnations in January? I had to drive two hours down the coast and back. I almost missed her train."

"That's what he gave her when they first met," Katie explained to Sierra, "a dozen white carnations. She was only . . ." Katie turned to Christy. "How old were you? Fourteen?"

"No, it was right after my birthday. I was fifteen."

"Anyway," Katie continued, as if Sierra were the only

one around, "Todd gave her white carnations when they met almost four years ago, and she has kept them all this time in a Folgers coffee can. They're all brown and withered, and they smell gross."

"They do not," Christy protested.

"You kept those?" Todd asked. He slipped his arm around Christy's shoulder and gave it a squeeze.

"I almost tossed them out a couple of times," Christy confessed. "But I still have them. And they *don't* smell." She made a face at Katie.

"Trust me," Katie said to Sierra, "they smell like moldy coffee. But that's not the point here. It's the bracelet. See, Todd gave her that forever bracelet for Christmas—"

"It was actually on New Year's three years ago," Tracy corrected. "Right after the party at my house."

"Okay, so New Year's," Katie said.

Doug interrupted with, "All Todd gave me that year was the book, *101 Things to Do With a Dead Hamster.* You remember that?"

"Yes!" Christy and Tracy said in unison. They didn't appear to have as many fond memories of the book as Doug and Todd seemed to.

Doug and Todd both had their arms around their girlfriends but managed to slap each other a high five in memory of the dead hamster book.

"Will you guys let me finish!" Katie said, stomping her foot. "So, you see, Sierra, they've been pretty much together, sort of, for the past three years. But then Todd received this letter to go full time with some mission organization, but he didn't want to go because he and Christy were getting so close."

"It was really because I didn't want to have to sell Gus, my VW bus."

Katie continued, ignoring Todd's sarcastic comment. "But Christy broke up with him. She let him go, no strings attached, so he could serve God full time. It was the most noble act the world has ever seen. I'm not exaggerating. And when they broke up, she gave him back the bracelet. Todd said if they ever got back together again, it would be because God had done it. He said if he ever put that bracelet on her wrist again, it would be forever!"

"If I ever suffer a memory lapse, I'm coming to you, Katie," Todd teased. "You seem to know my life better than I do."

"I didn't know he was in Spain," Christy explained to Sierra. "I thought the mission had sent him to Papua New Guinea because that's where he always wanted to go."

"The need was greater in Spain," Todd explained. "Once I went through the training, it became clear God wanted me to go to Castelldefels. It didn't hurt a bit that the surfing there is pretty decent." A grin crept onto Todd's face.

Christy went on. "Todd didn't know I was in England or coming to Spain until he received a fax the day before I arrived, explaining who he was supposed to meet at the train station. That's why this is such a shock to everybody. We couldn't have planned getting back together like this. God did it. And we had such a fantastic week of ministry!"

"I want to hear all about it," Tracy said. "Is that the dinner bell?"

They all paused to listen. It was indeed time for dinner.

"I need to wash up," Sierra said. She felt as if she needed to walk away from all of them. The sooner, the better. "I'm glad to meet you, Todd. And Christy, I'm really happy for you. For both of you. That's amazing how God worked it all out. I'll see you guys at dinner."

Sierra was about to slip out when Todd reached over and gently grasped her shoulder. "Sit by us at dinner, okay?"

"Okay," Sierra said, not sure why he was being so nice to her. She made her way into the nearest bathroom and, locking the door behind her, turned on the water and splashed her face two, three, four times. With each splash her tears mingled with the chilly water and washed down the drain.

"This is stupid," Sierra muttered to herself. "Why are you crying?" She looked at herself in the mirror above the sink. "I'm happy for Christy. I really am. And for Tracy and Doug too. Am I so self-centered that I can't share their happiness just because I didn't meet anybody on this trip? That is so immature, and I hate myself for even thinking it!"

Sierra washed her face again and commanded the

tears to cease. She was surprised when they obeyed. Smiling at her reflection, Sierra felt her confidence returning. She had never felt so overwhelmed by her emotions.

Maybe I wanted to cry like everyone else was because I was happy for Christy, but I didn't feel I could because I'm not part of their group. I mean, I am, but only for a week. They have been friends forever. Forever. Just like her bracelet. Will there ever be anyone who will promise to love me forever?

Sierra took a deep breath and ran a finger through the wet, matted curls around her forehead. *They're all older than I,* she reasoned. *Christy and Katie are two years older; Doug's five years older; and Todd must be at least four or five years older. So why am I comparing myself to them? They're all in college, and I still have a year and a half of high school. I knew it would be awkward on this trip being one of the youngest. I guess I thought I was mature enough to handle it.*

She smiled again and adjusted one of her earrings. If Todd was the kind of guy she thought he was, he would save a seat for her at dinner. She would sit with Christy and Todd and all their friends—make that, all her friends—and she would be just as mature as they were. And if all else failed, she would pull her chair next to Katie. She and Katie could always call an emergency meeting of the P.O. Club and go off together and sulk.

chapter three

SIERRA ACTUALLY HAD A GOOD TIME AT dinner. The conversation switched from all the love stories and turned into an equal-opportunity sharing time. Sierra felt like one of the group again. She sat next to Katie on one side and Doug on the other. Christy and Todd were across the table from them.

A couple of times Sierra caught Christy and Todd giving each other heart-stopping looks of admiration and mutual affection. It reminded Sierra of her brother. Cody had been enamored with his wife, Katrina, all through high school. They started going together when they were sophomores and were married right out of high school, with the blessing of both sets of parents. Cody and Katrina were meant for each other. It was obvious to everyone. They were still intensely in love, even after being married six years. They had an adorable little boy, Tyler.

Maybe I want it to be easy for me, like that. Maybe I feel behind since Cody was so in love when he was my age.

"I can't believe I'm saying this," Katie said toward the end of dinner, "but being around you guys like this is making me homesick."

"You miss your family?" Todd asked.

"Maybe a little bit. I'm mostly homesick for being young again. You know, going to the beach and everything we did together. Our high school years were the best. Don't you think so? I don't know how we got so old so fast."

"I know what you mean," Christy agreed. "My brother, David, is thirteen. I don't know when he grew up. He's somehow turned into this lanky teenager, and I hardly know who he is. He answered the phone when I called this afternoon, and I had no idea it was him. My baby brother! All grown up!"

"Well, almost grown up," Katie said. "David will always be a little dweeb in my book."

"What about you, Katie?" Sierra asked. "Do you have brothers or sisters?"

"Two older brothers. They're both big dweebs."

"And you, Todd?" This was the answer she was most interested in. What if Todd had a brother a few years younger? Someone just like him, only closer to Sierra's age.

"None. I'm the only kid. What about you, Sierra?"

"Four brothers and one sister."

"You have six kids in your family?" Doug asked. "Do you guys wear name tags to keep everyone straight?"

"Of course not! Six isn't a lot. My dad came from a

family of nine kids. I have two older brothers. The oldest one is in college, and the next one is married and
works construction. My sister is two years older than I,
and then there's Dillon and Gavin. They're eight and six."

"Sounds like your mom kind of did kids in pairs," Katie
said. "At least you each had someone your own gender
to share a room with."

"I hate sharing a room. Tawni is super picky about
everything. Whenever I have a really good dream, it
always involves me *not* having to share a room with
Tawni."

"Do you guys all have cowboy names?" Katie said.

"They're not cowboy names," Sierra said.

"Okay, then western names. What's your oldest brother's name?"

"Wes."

Everyone started to laugh.

"No, wait, you guys!" Sierra held up her hands, trying to get their attention. "That's just his nickname. His
real name is Wesley. That's because Wesley was my
mom's maiden name. She's related to Charles and John
Wesley, who were famous Christians a long time ago."

"And your next brother?" Katie prodded, on a hunt
for more cowboy names and not at all impressed with
Sierra's family history.

"My married brother's name is Cody."

Again everyone laughed.

"See? They're all cowboy names. What does your dad
do? Run a ranch or something?" Katie said.

"No," Sierra said, and now she started to giggle.

"What does he do?"

"You're going to laugh. My dad was a county sheriff."

They laughed with Sierra, and Christy asked, "Did he have a silver badge and everything?"

Sierra nodded and wiped the laughter tears from her eyes. "I guess we are a bit on the western side. I never thought of it before. I always thought of us as Danish, since that's where my Grandma is from."

"What's her name?" Christy asked.

"Mae. Mae Jensen. We call her Granna Mae. I do have her name as my middle name, if that counts for anything. Mae's not a western name, is it?"

Christy shrugged. "I don't think so."

"What's your middle name?" Sierra asked Christy.

Christy looked at Todd with a shy smile. "It's Juliet."

Now everyone was laughing, especially Doug.

"All right, Douglas!" Tracy said with a hand on her hip. "If you think that's so funny, tell everyone your middle name."

Doug turned sober. Tracy's eyebrows rose. "Would you like me to tell them?"

Doug quietly said, "Quinten."

Another round of laughter followed as Doug tried to explain that it was a family name, just like Mae and Wesley, and there was nothing funny about it at all.

By the time the six of them left the dining room and headed for the chapel for the evening meeting, they had laughed themselves silly. All of them were weary from their travels, which made them all the sillier. Especially Katie.

Sierra couldn't believe how fast Katie's mind seemed to be working, providing a funny response to everything everyone said. It was going to be hard to come back down to earth in chapel.

The assistant director of Carnforth Hall stood at the chapel's back door and greeted each of the students. When Sierra arrived with her group, he grasped Todd by the arm and said, "Dr. Benson had to go to a funeral in Edinburgh so I'm heading this up. Have you guys got the music covered?"

"We're all set," Todd said. He let go of Christy's hand, and he and Doug headed toward the front of the chapel. Sierra sat next to Christy, Tracy, and Katie. It was back to just the girls, and it was kind of nice.

Four guys were up front with guitars, and Todd seemed to be in charge. Since Todd and Doug were so wired from dinner, they started off the music with three rowdy, hand-clapping songs. They got the whole roomful of students singing and clapping. It seemed that all the returning groups were pretty keyed up.

Sierra loved it. Her little church back in Pineville was pretty conservative. They would never have been so vigorous in their worship.

After the fourth song, the assistant director came to the microphone and asked everyone to sit down. "Before we move into the worship and praise portion of chapel, I wanted to make a few announcements. First, I'd like to introduce Todd Spencer here on the guitar."

Todd smiled and gave a casual chin-up gesture to the group of forty or so gathered in the chapel.

"Todd is our mission director in Spain. He's on a two-year commitment, working with the teen outreach at Castelldefels. Todd is also completing his college degree by correspondence. When his term is up with the mission a year from this June, he'll have a B.A. in intercultural studies. If any of you are interested in finishing up your degree while in full-time ministry, see me, and I'll get you all the necessary information." He looked back at Doug and the other guys playing guitar. "Was there anything else? Doug? Were you the one who said you had an announcement?"

Doug shook his head.

Katie, who was sitting next to Sierra, suddenly blurted out, "Doug wanted to announce that his middle name is Quinten!" At first people around the room didn't laugh. They all looked at Doug, who took it good-naturedly. He gave Katie a thumbs up gesture and then threw back his head and laughed. The rest of the room joined as the assistant director shook his head. "It's always the Americans," he said in the microphone.

Katie leaned over to Sierra and said, "I've been waiting for that one for a long time. Ever since Doug gave me a black eye right before the first day of my senior year in high school."

The crowd settled down as Todd began to strum a set of familiar chords on his guitar that led into a moderately lively song. Soon the group was singing as one, song after song. They went from fast tempo to slower. Then a hush settled over the room as they prayerfully sang the final chorus. Sierra closed her eyes and sang from her heart, listening to her voice blend perfectly with Christy's and Tracy's.

A time of prayer followed in which people spontaneously thanked God for what had happened with their teams in the cities they had just returned from. Many of them prayed by name for people they had met. Sierra prayed for an elderly woman in Belfast who said she believed she would get to heaven simply because she was a good person. She had refused to believe she needed to trust Christ for her salvation. Something in the woman's appearance or mannerisms had reminded Sierra of Granna Mae, only Granna Mae was one of the strongest Christians Sierra had ever met.

The group prayed and shared for more than an hour. Reports of all that God had done among them during the past week were amazing.

After the meeting Katie and Sierra went to the main hall where their luggage was still sitting in the entryway. They hauled it up to their room and settled in for the night.

"Doesn't it seem like a couple of years have passed since we were in this room last?" Katie asked.

"I know," Sierra agreed. "And it's only been a week."

"It's really going to seem weird when we go home. We've changed so much in just a few short weeks. Probably everything at home will be exactly the same," Katie said.

"For you maybe," Sierra said with a laugh, crawling into her bed and rubbing her legs up and down against the sheets, trying to warm them. "Brrr! I forgot how cold this room is."

"What do you mean 'for me'? Don't you think everything will be the same in your family?" Katie asked, pulling her bed closer to Sierra's before climbing in and pulling the thick covers up to her chin.

"Well, you see, Katie, when I left a few weeks ago, my family moved. I've heard of parents trying to drop hints to their children about leaving the nest, but my parents are a little extreme."

"You're kidding, right?"

"Not exactly. They really did move. That was one of the reasons they agreed to my coming on this trip in the middle of the school year. I'll start my new school at the beginning of the semester."

Katie fluffed up her pillow and said, "What did you do, ace all your finals early?"

"Sort of. The high school I went to in Pineville was really small. I would have been in a graduating class of fifty-seven. Only two hundred students are in the whole high school. All my teachers were real nice and let me take exams early."

Just then the door opened, and Christy and Tracy entered, giggling about something. Katie looked over at Sierra and raised her eyebrows. "The Juliets have returned from their Romeos."

"Did you girls have a good time?" Sierra said in her best motherly voice.

"I'm sorry," Tracy said. "Are we being totally obnoxious?"

"Only partially obnoxious," Sierra teased. "I guess that's what Katie and I have to look forward to when we fall in love some day."

"Yeah, some day," Katie quipped. "Like when I'm eighty-five, and some old guy at the rest home starts to chase me around in his wheelchair."

"Oh, do you think it will happen that soon?" Sierra teased. "That's encouraging. I might still have some of my original teeth!"

"You guys shouldn't be so sarcastic," Christy warned, sitting on the edge of her bed and slipping off her shoes. "Love can hit you when you least expect it."

"Oh really?" Katie said, sitting up in bed and nimbly pulling out her pillow. "Like this?" She whacked Christy on the side of the head. Christy let out a startled shriek and immediately retaliated by tossing her pillow at Katie. But she missed and hit Sierra in the face. Sierra sprang into action. Then Tracy grabbed her pillow, and it was a free-for-all.

The four friends squealed like little kids and whacked each other silly until Sierra's pillow burst open and tiny white feathers fluttered everywhere. They were laughing so hard they were crying and fanning the floating feathers away from their faces.

A brisk knock on the door turned into several solid thumps. The girls squelched their laughter.

"Yes?" Sierra called out in a controlled voice.

"Ladies?" The deep male voice called through the

closed door. "What on earth is going on in there? We can hear you in the south wing of the castle!"

"Um, we were just laughing, sir, but we're going to bed now," Sierra answered, still maintaining her straight face.

"Good night then, ladies. Lights out."

"Yes, good night, sir," Sierra said, reaching over and switching off the light. They listened as the footsteps echoed down the hallway and then turned the light back on.

"Very impressive," Katie said, brushing her red hair out of her eyes. "How did you do that?"

"I grew up in a big family, remember? I've had a lot of practice. What you really have to do is learn how to have silent pillow fights."

Christy flopped down on her bed and stared at the ceiling. "Truce, you guys. I can't take another round, silent or otherwise. I don't think I've ever laughed so hard or so much in my whole life as I have today. It's good to be back together!"

Tracy started to clean up the feathers.

"Let's leave them until tomorrow," Sierra said. "It'll be easier to clean up in the morning. I think there's another pillow in the closet I can use."

"I'll get it for you," Tracy said, walking across the room. "I feel bad about the mess."

"Don't worry. It'll still be a mess in the morning," Sierra said. "That's what I always tell my sister, but she's so picky. Everything has to be in place before she can allow herself to go to bed."

Tracy stepped out of the closet and handed a pillow to Sierra. "Does anybody else need anything while I'm up?"

There was no answer.

"Christy, can you change in the dark if I turn off the light?"

Silence.

"I think she's asleep," Katie said, settling back under her covers.

Sierra peeked up over her blanket, and sure enough, Christy was asleep on her back with a smile on her lips. "Tracy, we better try to get her under the blankets. She's going to freeze like that," Sierra said.

Tracy, ever the helpful type, spoke softly to Christy, coaxing her to roll over enough for Sierra to pull up the blankets and wrap them around her. Christy cooperated but seemed as if she were doing so in her sleep.

Within minutes they were all tucked in bed. One lone feather fluttered through the air and landed on Sierra's cheek. She batted it away and slipped off into dreamland.

chapter four

SIERRA DIDN'T WAKE UP THE NEXT morning until almost ten o'clock. The other girls were still asleep when she opened her eyes, and the floor was still covered with a carpet of feathers. Sierra tiptoed to the hall closet and returned with a broom. Quietly she cleaned up the feathers without waking the others.

She could hear voices in the room next door. Some of the other girls were starting to wake up. Anticipating the exhaustion, the mission directors had forgone breakfast and were offering a buffet brunch from ten to noon. Sierra decided to quickly shower while some hot water remained.

By the time she finished and returned to the room, the other three girls were awake and trying to get themselves going.

"I can't believe how tired I am," Christy said. "I can't remember ever falling asleep with my clothes still on!"

"Do you mind waiting for us, Sierra?" Tracy asked. "We can all go to brunch together."

"I don't mind. Take your time." Sierra towel-dried her wild, caramel-colored hair and pulled on her boots. She opened a zippered pouch on the inside of her suitcase and fished for a matching pair of earrings. Today she chose the ones with the moon and stars suspended from thin silver chains. She searched for her silver hoop bracelets, eight of them all looped together, and pushed them up her left arm. Around her neck hung a string of tiny multicolored beads that looked like bits of confetti against her forest green knit shirt. She felt refreshed after her shower, hungry, and ready for that brunch.

She didn't mind waiting for the others, though. It gave her a chance to read her Bible, which she pulled from her brown leather backpack. The medium-sized book was covered with a handmade, tooled-leather cover that her dad had made for her years ago. The design was of a tree that, at the bottom of its trunk, had "Psalm 1:3" embossed.

That had been Sierra's favorite verse as a kid, which she had memorized in second grade. This morning she turned to the book of Psalms and picked up where she had left off reading a few days ago, at Psalm 62.

Verse eight really stood out to her: "Trust in Him at all times, you people; pour out your heart before Him; God is a refuge for us."

Sierra thought of how she had been holding in her discomfort about the move to Portland. She hadn't poured her heart out to anyone, not even God.

The door opened right then, and Sierra's roommates

returned, all three wearing towels wrapped around their heads. They stood in the doorway with goofy looks on their faces. On Katie's signal they all held their right hands out in front of them, wiggled their hips, and sang in their most soulful voices, "Stop! In the name of love!"

Sierra started to laugh, and pretty soon the three soul sisters were giggling so hard their "beehive" towel-dos came tumbling down.

"Hurry up, you goofs," Sierra said. "It's almost eleven thirty. They're going to close down the buffet before we get there!"

About fifteen minutes later, they all descended on the dining room. Sierra filled her plate and ate every bite. Just as Mrs. Bates was clearing away all the food, Doug and Todd walked in.

"Those two are going to be sorry they slept in," Christy said.

It looked as if Todd was sweet-talking Mrs. Bates into letting them scrape the bottom of all the serving bowls for whatever was left.

Tracy giggled as they watched the guys coax the pan of ham slices out from underneath Mrs. Bates's protective arm. Todd stuffed hard-boiled eggs into the front pouch pocket of his navy blue hooded sweatshirt while Doug snatched a basket of rolls from the serving table and held it behind his back. "She doesn't realize those two will eat anything," Tracy said, "especially Doug. She could let them empty out all the leftovers in her refrigerator, and they'd be just as happy."

The guys, with their arms full of loot and expressions of brave conquerors across their shaven faces, joined the girls.

"You guys get the bamboozle award for the day," Katie said. "I think you two could hoodwink even the Queen Mother if she were here today!"

Doug and Todd gave each other mischievous smiles.

"What?" Christy asked. "I know that look. What did you guys do?"

"Oh, nothing," Doug said.

Todd poured himself a glass of juice and tried to repress his chuckling.

"Tell us!" Tracy demanded.

The grin on Todd's face kept growing. He avoided eye contact with Christy and lifted the glass of apple juice to his lips.

Doug looked as if he were about to burst. He glanced at Todd and then at Tracy. Looking directly at Katie, he furrowed his eyebrows and said in an extra deep voice, "Ladies, what on earth is going on in there? We can hear you in the south wing of the castle!"

Katie's mouth dropped open.

"Good night, then, ladies," Doug continued. "Lights out!"

"It was you!?" Katie rose from her seat with both hands outstretched, ready to strangle Doug.

Todd started to laugh so hard that the apple juice squirted out his nose. He grabbed a napkin, rose from the table, and turned his back to the group until he could stop coughing.

"You guys are so immature!" Katie squawked, plopping back down in her seat and folding her arms across her chest. "It's as if your little brains froze at about the level of twelve-year-olds. I can't believe you guys!"

"Us!?" Todd said, regaining his voice sans any stray liquids. "And just what were you *mature* women doing last night? It sounded like an all-out, junior-high-style pillow fight to me!"

"It was," Sierra said, laughing with the rest of them. "Too bad you guys weren't in on it. We would have creamed you!"

"Oh, yeah?" Doug said. "Would you like us to take you up on that challenge tonight? Huh?"

"I dare you!" Sierra said, rising to her feet and sticking her chin out at Doug the way she had done many times with her older brothers.

Katie jumped to her feet beside Sierra and said, "Yeah, we dare you!"

"Tonight," Doug said, pointing a finger at Katie and Sierra and trying to look tough. "We'll be there."

"Yeah," said Todd, echoing Doug's macho voice, "tonight!"

Dr. Benson stepped into the dining room and announced that chapel would begin in fifteen minutes. He looked tired. Sierra remembered he had been at a funeral in Scotland. Perhaps he had just arrived.

In chapel the guys played guitar again, and for the first half hour they sang, which Sierra loved. Then Dr. Benson gave a talk about adjusting to life when they returned home. He instructed each of the students to take his or her Bible and find a place to read, pray, and prepare for returning home.

Sierra chose a bench at the back of the chapel. Nearly everyone else had filed out, except three or four people who were scattered around the chapel having their own quiet time with the Lord. She read her chapter again from that morning and prayed.

"You say You want me to pour my heart out to You, God. Well, here goes. I'm scared. Yeah, me. Scared. Doesn't happen too often, but I am. I didn't want to move. I don't want to go to a new school. Not that I don't want to meet new people. It's just that I guess I liked being sort of popular at Pineville High. Now I'm going to be nobody. And that's okay, if that's who You want me to be. But I feel intimidated by it all, and You know it takes a lot to intimidate me. As long as I'm pouring out my heart here, the other thing that's driving me crazy is the way everyone is getting a boyfriend, and I'm not. These guys are really solid, quality guys. I'm afraid there won't be any more like them left for me. I know I'm supposed to trust You . . ."

Sierra opened her eyes and peeked at verse eight again: "Trust in Him at all times."

"Okay," she prayed, "so I'm supposed to trust in You at all times, even in boyfriend-less times, and I *am* trying. But I would like You to make note that I am sweet sixteen and never been kissed. I haven't even had my hand held. Can You see how that would make someone

like me feel a little insecure about her looks and personality and everything? Just so You understand, which
I know You do."

Feeling surrendered, Sierra left the chapel and took
one last walk around the grounds. She kept talking
silently with God as she walked.

Sierra talked with God like this often. She had given
her heart to Jesus when she was five and had continued
a close walk with Him ever since. It had been fairly easy
in her strong Christian family and in the safe community of Pineville. She knew challenges lay ahead for her
in Portland.

That evening after dinner, Sierra and her team gathered together one last time. Last night there had been
unstoppable laughter. Tonight the tears began and
didn't seem to stop. Even after the girls were in bed with
the lights off, they kept talking and crying and making
promises to stay in close contact with each other. With
the flood of emotions, everyone forgot about the challenge of the pillow fight.

The next morning, even though Sierra thought she
had emptied herself of all her good-bye tears the night
before, she cried when she joined the group on the 5:00
A.M. shuttle van to the train station. It was still dark
outside and very cold. Everyone in her group was up
and dressed to see her off.

Sierra received endless hugs from her friends. Katie
hugged her first and said, "Somehow it's not so hard
saying good-bye to you because I know I'm going to see

you again. We'll get together this summer, if not before."

Todd even hugged her good-bye, and when he did, he said, "I guess we'll have to reschedule that pillow fight."

"Okay," Sierra agreed. The tears welled up in her eyes. She knew she might never see Todd or Doug again, and the promised pillow fight was an empty threat.

Christy hugged her the last of everyone and said, "I hold you in my heart, Sierra. I always will." The two young women held each other at arm's length, and each wiped away the other's tears. Christy then placed her hand on Sierra's forehead and said, "Sierra, may the Lord bless you and keep you. The Lord make His face to shine upon you and give you His peace. And may you always love Jesus first, above all else."

Sierra waved and stepped up into the van. The rest of them were going to London that afternoon and staying overnight at a boarding house. Their flights went out early the next morning with Doug, Tracy, and Christy flying into Los Angeles and Todd flying to Barcelona. Sierra hated being the first one to leave. "Good-bye, you guys!" she called out and waved one last time.

Even with such a blessing and send-off, Sierra felt as if a dark cloud had settled over her head and hung there all the way to Heathrow Airport. She stood in line at the ticket counter, checked her bag, and asked directions to her gate. Everything was going smoothly. Her plane was scheduled to leave in an hour.

She decided to call her mom and dad and let them

know she was on schedule. Sierra had to fumble through her backpack to find her new phone number. It felt weird not knowing her own number by heart.

When she located the phones, they were all in use so Sierra stood patiently to the side and waited her turn. A guy on the second phone turned around and, noticing Sierra standing there, put his hand over the receiver and said, "Excuse me, but do you have any coins? I'm desperate!"

By his accent, she knew he was American. "I'm not sure." Sierra hurriedly opened her backpack and rummaged around the bottom of the bag for any loose coins. She walked over to the frantic-looking guy and handed him four coins. Then she searched for more.

"You're a lifesaver!" he whispered as he fed the coins into the phone. "Yes, this is Paul. Is Jalene there?" He motioned for more coins. Sierra struck pay dirt in the zippered pouch on the front of her backpack and pulled out nine of them. She wasn't sure what they were, how much they were worth, or how much she had just given away to this stranger. He eagerly received her gift and fed the money into the phone.

"Hi! I only have a minute on this phone," he said. "Let me give you my flight number. Are you ready? It's flight 931 to San Francisco and then flight 57 to Portland. Have you got that?"

Sierra took a few steps back and nonchalantly looked at her ticket. She was on the same flights.

"I arrive in Portland at 8:24 P.M. Got it? Great! Okay,

I'll see you then. Thanks a lot. Bye!" He pulled the
phone away from his ear and held it out to Sierra. "Just
enough," he said. She could hear the dial tone. "I owe
you. How much did you give me?"

"I have no idea," Sierra admitted. As she spoke, she
took a good look at "Paul" for the first time. He had
thick, dark brown hair that had a natural wave at the top
of his broad forehead. He wore a tan leather jacket and
attached to his backpack was an Indiana-Jones-style hat.

Sierra was surprised to find herself thinking, *Fight
for this man.*

"I'll pay you back in dollars," he said, reaching into
his pocket.

"Sorry," said a man next to Sierra with a British
accent. "Are you waiting for that phone?"

"Yes, I am." Sierra stepped forward and took the
phone from Paul and began to place a collect call to her
parents. Paul stood next to her, still scrounging for the
money to pay her back. He acted as if they were
together. Sierra held the receiver in place with her
shoulder. She could smell a strong, earthy cologne. She
guessed it to be Paul's.

Sierra's dad answered the phone, and she spoke in
low tones, leaning into the phone, fully aware that this
guy stood only a few feet away, waiting for her. She
assured her dad that everything was fine and on schedule. He promised to be at the gate to meet her when she
deplaned. "I love you, too," Sierra said softly and then
hung up.

She turned around and met Paul's eyes. They were gray. No, they were blue. No, they looked gray. And very clear, like water. "I only have two dollars on me," he said. "Do you mind following me over to the money exchange booth? I can cash a traveler's check and pay you back. Is that okay? Are you in a hurry?"

"All right," Sierra said, shrugging her shoulders. "I'll follow you."

"My name's Paul," he said. "I apologize for presuming on you. You were very kind to help me out. Thanks."

"It's okay. Don't worry about it."

They stood in line at the money exchange booth. Sierra felt Paul staring at her. When she couldn't stand the sensation any longer, she turned and looked at him. He didn't turn away or act embarrassed.

"You don't wear any makeup, do you?" Paul noted.

Now Sierra felt really odd. This guy was blunt. That was her usual approach, and it had gotten her in trouble more than once. "No, do you?" she countered playfully.

Paul looked shocked at first and then a delighted smile inched onto his face. "Not that you need to or anything."

Sierra leaned a bit closer to him, as if scrutinizing his complexion right back. "And neither do you," she said flatly.

This time Paul laughed.

They were up to the window now, and Sierra stood to the side as he pulled out his passport and wrote out a traveler's check. The clerk counted the money back to him and slid it on the metal tray under the glass window.

"Here you go," Paul said, stepping away from the window and handing Sierra a twenty-dollar bill.

"I don't have change for a twenty."

"All I have is twenties," he said. "You'll have to take it."

"But then I'll owe you," Sierra said.

"Don't worry about it." He looked at his watch. "Hey, thanks again. I have a plane to catch."

"Me too," Sierra said as he dashed away, his backpack flung over his shoulder.

Sierra began to hike to her flight gate, a few yards behind Paul. She thought about calling out to him and walking with him since she knew they were on the same flight. But something held her back, which was not typical of her. Usually she could approach anyone at any time.

She watched him as she waited to check in at the ticket counter. Paul was ahead of her in line, with three rather large people in between them. Paul never turned around. He left the waiting area as soon as he checked in and returned only when they called the flight. Sierra was standing by the window and watched him get in line to board the plane.

This is so ridiculous! What am I doing watching this guy?

Sierra entered the single-file line of passengers with her ticket in hand and her backpack over her shoulder.

She watched the well-worn hat looped over the top of Paul's leather backpack as he shuffled through the line. About eight people were between them this time.

A crazy thought danced through her imagination. *What if our seats are next to each other?*

Sierra smiled at the flight attendant and made her way to the rear of the plane. She could still see Paul's bobbing hat down the aisle in front of her. It was a good sign; he hadn't reached his seat yet. Only a few more and he would be at her row. Suddenly Paul stopped. Sierra held her breath.

chapter five

*S*IERRA WATCHED AS PAUL SLUNG HIS
backpack off his shoulder and ducked his head
beneath the overhead compartment. He hadn't
seemed so tall at the phones in the terminal but now he
seemed not only tall but also broad-shouldered. Of
course, since Sierra was five foot five and a half most
guys did seem tall to her. She checked her seat number
again.

*Rats! I'm three rows behind him. Will he notice me
when I walk by?*

Sierra slowly shuffled past him. Paul had his head
down, stuffing his backpack under the seat in front of
him. She lingered just a minute, wondering if she
should say something. He straightened up but kept his
eyes lowered as he adjusted his seat belt.

Aware of the line of people behind her, Sierra made
her way to her row and slid in next to the window. An
older gentleman sat in the aisle seat.

Why couldn't this have been Paul's place? she thought,
looking at the vacant middle seat between her and the

older man. *Then again, he didn't have anyone next to him yet. Maybe I should think of an excuse to go up and casually sit by him, as if I think that spot is mine. No, too cheesy. Maybe I should slip out and search for a pillow or magazine or something and see if he notices me when I walk past. Let him make the first move. I'll stand there, chatting nonchalantly with him, then the stewardess will come by and tell me to take my seat. I'll have to sit down right then and there! What am I thinking? This is ridiculous.*

"Good day to you," said the man in the aisle seat. He was bald with little round glasses. His hands were contentedly folded across his round middle, and his short legs were stretched out and crossed at the ankles. He looked awfully comfortable, and Sierra couldn't bear to ask him if she could slide past him to parade down the aisle. She returned his greeting and then gazed out the window.

A luggage tram pulled up next to the plane, and two men began to toss bags onto a conveyor belt that inched its way up into the plane's belly. Sierra thought she would prefer to ride in the cargo with the luggage than to have to spend the next fifteen hours peering over three rows of seats to spy on the back of Paul's head.

Reaching for a magazine in the seat pocket in front of her, Sierra forced herself to think about something else. She flipped through the pages, pretending to scan the articles. Her mind felt mushy. She had no idea what time it was or how much longer it would be before the plane took off.

The flight attendant made her way down the aisle, checking seat belts and offering pillows and blankets. Sierra accepted both. Suddenly she felt sleepy. A nap before dinner would do her good. She pulled the blanket up under her chin and balanced the pillow behind her neck.

Closing her eyes, she tried to sort out all the thoughts, feelings, and experiences of the past few weeks. This was the first time she had been alone for any significant time the entire trip. Maybe it was good she wasn't trying to carry on a conversation with Paul.

The plane taxied down the runway and took off. Sierra looked out her window. In less than a minute the nose of the plane pierced the thick blanket of fog that hung over Heathrow Airport, and all Sierra could see was a shroud of gray. She tried to catch a glimpse of Paul ahead of her. Was he looking out the window too? Was he reading? Sleeping? She reclined her seat, closed her eyes, and went back to categorizing and filing the events of her trip.

Sierra felt herself begin to doze off. Then, just for good measure, she moved her pillow over to the window and leaned against it with her face open to the aisle. Actually, she was more comfortable with the pillow behind her head and her chin down. But her hair fell across the side of her face in that position. This way, if Paul *did* happen to walk by, he would certainly notice her. She only hoped she wouldn't start drooling while she slept.

When Sierra next opened her eyes, the flight attendant was offering her a dinner tray. She lowered her tray table, adjusted herself in her seat, and tried to shake awake enough to eat. A movie followed that Sierra tried to watch, but she fell asleep again and dozed uncomfortably off and on for many hours.

At one point she shifted in her seat and noticed the man in the aisle seat was gone. She decided to use the opportunity to go to the restroom at the rear of the plane. Several people stood back there in the cramped quarters, waiting for one of the four restroom doors to open. Sierra stood with them, yawning and glancing around.

Paul was standing only six feet away by the small serving area, asking the stewardess for something to drink. Once again, Sierra was paralyzed. Paul wasn't looking at her. He seemed oblivious to her existence. Why should she be so interested in him? Thanking the stewardess, Paul accepted the beverage and started to return to his seat. Then suddenly he turned and looked back over his shoulder in Sierra's direction.

This was the encounter she had been waiting for. And what did she do? She immediately turned her head away and studied the silver "occupied" sign on the bathroom door in front of her.

What a dork I am! Did he notice me? Did he know I was here, and was he looking back to see if I had recognized him? I guess I'll never know, will I?

Sierra chanced a peek over her shoulder through a

wild mass of her unruly curls. He was gone. Now she had to make those silly, cat-and-mouse decisions all over again. Should she return to her seat by walking the long way around the plane so she could saunter past his seat and they might make eye contact?

She entered the tiny restroom and took a look in the mirror. "Night of the Flying Zombies," she muttered to herself. Her eyes were puffy, and across her right cheek was a deep crease from the pillow. At least she didn't have to be concerned about mascara smears.

Sierra thought back on Stephen's comment to her and Katie a few days ago. He had said she was beautiful. Gorgeous. Her dad told her that all the time. But no *real* guy had ever said anything like that to her. Stephen didn't count because such a compliment would only matter if it came from an "eligible" guy, a guy whose opinion really mattered to her.

"So why do I think Paul is that kind of guy? Why am I so obsessed with him? This is getting out of control."

Sierra finished in the bathroom and returned to her seat by the most direct route, avoiding Paul. She crawled back under her blanket and silently prayed about her bothersome obsession. She didn't know if her unbridled thoughts about Paul were wrong or if they were normal. In either case, she knew it would be good to pray and surrender the whole thing to Christ. She remembered the verse she had read in Psalms about trusting in Him at all times and pouring out her heart to Him.

It worked. She felt more peace about Paul after praying. Only now all she could think about was arriving in
Portland in a few hours and everything being brand
new for her. She went right back to praying and pouring out her heart.

The plane landed on time in San Francisco. Sierra
knew she had to walk from the international terminal
over to another section where a much smaller plane
would take her to Portland exactly forty-two minutes
after this flight landed. It didn't leave much time for
customs.

Fortunately, Sierra hadn't bought many souvenirs
and had marked on her form that she had nothing to
declare. She was directed to a fast-moving line. Paul,
she noticed, wasn't in her line. She was tempted to turn
around and scan the crowd behind her but resisted the
urge. It was more important that she get her passport
cleared and find her way to the other end of the terminal to catch her next flight.

She made it with a few minutes to spare. Breathing
hard and feeling the perspiration beads form on her
forehead, Sierra settled into her seat and gazed out the
plane's window.

"Pardon me," a deep voice said. "I think you're in my
seat."

She turned to look into the surprised blue-gray eyes
of Paul. "It's you! How did you get here?" He said it
sincerely enough that Sierra believed he really didn't
know she had been on the flight from London.

"I swam," Sierra said with a smile, wiping the perspiration off her forehead and flipping her hair back over her shoulders.

Paul slid into the middle seat next to her, holding his backpack and hat on his lap. "Were we just on the same flight?"

She felt like saying, "Duh!" but instead she said, "As a matter of fact, we were."

"I wish I'd known," Paul said. He rose to put his gear in the overhead compartment and asked, "Do you want me to put anything up here for you?"

"No thanks," Sierra answered. She couldn't believe this was happening. Nearly sixteen hours ago in England she had hoped to sit next to Paul, then she had given up, and now here she and Paul were, and it all seemed so natural. "I didn't realize I was in the wrong seat," she said as he ducked to sit down. "Do you want the window seat?"

"No, that's fine. You deserve it. I feel as if I still owe you."

"You don't," Sierra said. "If anything, I owe you." She bent over, unzipped the outside pocket on her backpack, and pulled out a small white sack.

Once again she felt Paul staring at her. She could smell his aftershave, and it made her think of Christmas back in Pineville. This time she didn't try to catch him in his staring. Since this had developed into a most interesting turn of events, she decided to play it for all it was worth. Let him stare. What did he see? Was he deciding she was worth pursuing?

Even as she entertained these thoughts, Sierra felt guilty. What a flirting game! She knew nothing about this guy except that his name was Paul, he was going to Portland, and he was gutsy enough to beg money from a stranger but honorable enough to pay it back with interest.

Now it was her turn to pay back with interest. "I still don't have any change," she said, holding out the sack and smiling at him. "But will you take this? It's chocolates from Finland."

Paul raised an eyebrow and peered at the crumpled bag. "Chocolate?"

"Here," Sierra offered. "Consider it change for your twenty."

Paul accepted the gift and reached into the sack. He took out one of the small cubes of chocolate and popped it in his mouth. "Oh, yeah," he said, closing his eyes. "Now *this* is chocolate! Where did you say it was from?"

"Finland."

"Is that where you've been?"

"No, I was in England and then in Ireland. One of the other girls in our group was from Finland, and she gave some to everyone the last day of our missions outreach."

Paul stopped sucking on the chocolate and looked closer at Sierra. "You weren't at Carnforth Hall, were you?"

"Yes, I was!"

"I don't believe it!" He leaned back his head and closed his eyes as if the news distressed him. Sierra peered closer at him, searching for a clue as to why that bothered him.

"Have you been there?" she ventured.

Paul looked at her, a normal expression returning to his face. "More times than I can count. My grandfather bought Carnforth Hall right after World War II. He used it to run summer Bible camps until about six years ago when he turned it over to the mission group that now operates it."

"You're kidding!"

Paul shook his head. "My grandfather just died. His funeral was in Edinburgh three days ago."

Sierra remembered that Dr. Benson had gone to Edinburgh for a funeral. "Was Dr. Benson there?"

"Charles? Yeah, he was there along with about eight hundred other people. My grandfather was a well-loved man." Paul looked contemplative and then switched to a less serious expression. "Did you meet a guy from San Diego named Doug at Carnforth?"

"Doug was my team leader! How do you know him?"

"He's friends with my older brother. My dad is the pastor at Mission Springs in El Cajon. Have you heard of it?"

Sierra shook her head. "Should I have?"

"It's a big church. Four thousand members. Doug goes there, and that's where he met my brother, Jeremy. They have this Sunday night group called God Lovers

that meets at Doug's apartment. I used to go there
when I was in high school. It was a big deal, hanging
out with all the college kids."

Sierra knew exactly what Paul meant. She had felt
that way this whole trip. "Did you ever meet a friend of
Doug's named Todd?"

"Surfer type? Plays guitar?"

"Yeah. He's the mission director now in Spain."

"Figures."

"Small world, isn't it?" Sierra replied.

"The circles in life are very small." Paul said it as if
he were quoting someone. "So, what brought you to
Carnforth?"

Sierra shrugged her shoulders. "God, I guess. I heard
about it from one of my cousins and decided to go."

Paul looked away. The plane was taking off. It was
much smaller and much noisier than the wide-body
had been from England.

Once they were airborne Sierra pursued their
conversation.

"Why are you going to Portland? Don't you live in
San Diego?"

"I'm going to school at L. and C."

Sierra looked at him as if the initials meant nothing.

"Lewis and Clark College." Paul reached in the white
bag and took out another chunk of chocolate. "Would
you like some of your own candy?"

Sierra took a small piece and thanked him. The
incredible chocolate melted in her mouth.

"You know what?" he said, lowering his voice and leaning a little closer. "I don't even know your name."

"Ah, but you know the really important stuff about me," Sierra said, feeling flirty. "Like I loan money to strangers, I don't wear makeup, and I'm generous with my world-class gourmet chocolate."

"True, true. And those are good qualities in a person. But what's your name?"

It was fun, stringing him along like this, but she decided to give in. "Sierra."

He gave her a peculiar look, as if her name pleased him, as if this were a test, and she had given the right answer. One hundred percent correct.

chapter six

"*S*IERRA," PAUL REPEATED HER NAME AS
if he were savoring it. "I like your boots."

She glanced down at her worn-out doggies
and said, "They're my dad's."

"And the quick wit?" Paul asked. "Is that your dad's
too?"

"As a matter of fact, it is," Sierra said.

"And you're going to Portland, because . . . ," Paul
waited for her to fill in the blank.

"Because I have a free place to eat and sleep there."

"Your parents' house?"

"Actually, my grandmother's house. My family moved
in with her while I was in England. It's a huge old
Victorian, and Granna Mae refused to sell it. She can't
keep it up or take care of herself anymore; so my dad
made a career change, and we all moved in with my
grandma."

"Sounds like something my dad would do. We grew
up in a pretty small house and always drove junker
cars. But every year my dad spent his saved-up pennies

55

on airline tickets so all five of us could spend the summer with our grandparents at Carnforth. Be glad that you can spend time with your grandmother now. It's a gift."

"I know," Sierra said. "She's my soul mate."

"Really?" said Paul. Once again he looked at Sierra as if she had given him the correct answer. "Most people don't feel that way about grandparents or elderly people in general. I was closer to my grandfather than to any other person I've ever known. It was like we had the same heart."

"And now that he's gone, how do you feel?" Sierra saw the hurt in Paul's face and the glistening in his eyes. She wanted to reach over and take his hand to comfort him.

"No one will ever take his place in my life. I feel as if I have a big hole right through the middle of me. At night, I can almost hear the wind whistling through it."

Sierra felt so connected with this poet of a man. Their eyes met, and neither of them said anything for a moment. Paul seemed to be staring deep inside her, drawing strength from her silence. She gazed back at him.

"Something to drink for you two?" the flight attendant asked, breaking their communion. They both turned to him, and at the same time said, "Orange juice with ice, please."

"Okay!" the uniformed man said with a laugh. "Two O.J.s on the rocks. Are you two brother and sister?"

Sierra and Paul looked blankly at each other and

then back at the flight attendant. "No, what made you think that?" Sierra asked.

"Your eyes. You have the same eyes." He moved on to the row behind them.

"Why did he say that?" Paul asked, turning back to look at Sierra.

"Beats me," she said, comically crossing her eyes and trying to stare at the freckles on her nose.

Paul laughed. "You don't suppose we really are twins, separated at birth, do you?"

"Not a chance. You're older," Sierra said.

"By how much? I was nineteen in December."

Sierra smiled and didn't answer.

"What? Are we about six months apart? Maybe nine?"

"Well, my birthday is November fourteenth . . ."

"You're kidding," Paul said. "That's my mom's birthday! So what, you were eighteen then?"

"No."

"Seventeen?"

"No."

"Sixteen?" he said slowly as Sierra nodded. "You're only sixteen?"

Sierra watched him physically draw back, and as he did, something changed between them. All the closeness evaporated. She wanted to defend herself, to tell him nothing was wrong with being sixteen, and actually she was mature for her age. But he was gone, closed off emotionally from whatever connection they had experienced.

They silently sipped their orange juice. "Is your boy-friend picking you up at the airport?" Paul suddenly asked.

"My boyfriend?"

"I heard you tell some guy on the phone in London that you loved him."

"That 'guy' was my dad."

"Oh," Paul looked at his plastic tumbler and said, "My girlfriend is picking me up."

"Oh," Sierra replied. "It's too bad she wasn't able to go to the funeral with you. I'm sure it would have been nice for you to have her there." Inside she felt all chewed up. Why was he telling her about his girlfriend? She could be mature about this, she coached herself. Just ask lots of questions.

"Actually, it wouldn't have been a good idea for her to have been there."

"Why?"

Paul swished the ice cubes around in his nearly empty cup. "Jalene is . . . well, she's different."

"You mean she's not a Christian," Sierra said.

Paul looked at her, startled at her discernment. "I didn't say that."

"You didn't have to."

A tense silence hung between them. Sierra was bugged. Why would a guy like Paul, with such a godly back-ground and all kinds of potential for ministry, fall for a girl who wasn't a Christian? She wanted to tell him exactly what she thought and realized she had nothing to lose. He obviously wasn't interested in her, not only because she was sixteen but also because he had a girlfriend. Sierra shifted into high gear.

"What are you doing with her? I mean, don't you see the potential for destruction in a relationship that's so lopsided? It's like a trap to get you to settle for less than God's best for your life."

Now Paul looked mad. "And where do you get off telling me what to do with my life? You think you're some prophetess or something? You don't know anything about me or my life or what God's best is for me!"

"And Jalene does?" Sierra asked. Tact had never been one of her strengths.

Paul looked really mad now. "What's it to you? Who do you think you are, anyway?" He looked away, as if the sight of her disgusted him.

Shaking his head, Paul fumbled for a magazine in the pouch in front of him and then reached up to turn on the light above his seat. Obviously he was shutting her out.

Sierra decided two could play this game. She swished her head away from him, pretending his behavior didn't bother her a bit. But one of her long, flying curls caught in the band of his wristwatch.

"Ouch!" Sierra tugged angrily to get free. It only tangled her hair more.

"Don't move," Paul snapped. "You're making it worse. Hold still."

Sierra couldn't see his face, but she could feel him pulling each thread of hair, releasing it from his watch.

"Man, you really torqued it in here." The angry edge seemed to subside from his voice. "I almost have it."

"Just pull it out," Sierra said stubbornly. "I don't care."

"Relax, will you? Now hold on. There. You're free. None the worse for wear."

Sierra smoothed down her ruffled mane but didn't turn to look at him.

"Thanks for the souvenir," Paul said.

She turned slightly to see what he meant. He was still pulling blond hairs from his watchband. "When you're caught like that it doesn't help to pull away." He sounded like Wesley when he was in one of his big-brother-advice-giving moods.

"Oh, right!" Sierra said, giving him a scolding look. "And you're one to tell me about jerking away! You can't even have a conversation about your girlfriend without pulling away."

Paul's reaction startled her. He started to laugh. It was deep, from the heart, merry laughter.

"What's so funny?" Sierra asked defensively. "You know I'm right."

"What are you?" Paul asked, still smiling. "My guardian angel or something?"

"I'm no angel."

"Some mystic warrior, then? Sent to guide me back to the right path?"

Sierra recalled the thought that had occurred to her when she first met Paul. *Fight for this man.* Maybe a battle was going on in his life. Maybe the Holy Spirit was calling her to be a prayer warrior for him. She had heard stories of people feeling compelled to pray for someone without knowing why. Later they had found out that God had used their prayers to redirect the course of that person's life.

"Maybe," she answered calmly. The whole chance encounter with this guy was a little too weird for her. "Just remember, you're the one who asked me for phone money. I wasn't trailing you, as you seem to think."

Paul looked at her again, studying her intensely. It didn't bother her. She felt open, with nothing to hide. What was it he was searching for?

"Sierra, you are an exceptional young woman. I pity the man who falls in love with you."

"And I pity any young woman who falls in love with you, if you're running away from God. Jonah tried that, remember? Unless you have an affection for whale barf, I'd encourage you to get your act together."

"Man!" Paul said, running his fingers through his dark, wavy hair. "You just don't quit, do you?"

Like an alarm going off in Sierra's head, she felt the call to retreat. She suddenly realized how brazen she was being.

"I'm sorry," Sierra said, looking down and feeling herself calm down. "I come on a little too strong sometimes. I apologize if I said anything out of line."

Paul raised an eyebrow. "From full-on in-your-face to innocent lamb. You do that very well. You must have some Scottish blood in you." A smile pulled up the corners of his mouth. "I imagine you'll grow into that zealous spirit. Right now I'd say it's a little too big for you."

It bothered Sierra that he was putting her down with such tender words. It bothered her that their intense conversation had gone nowhere. She had surrendered. What good had that done? She withdrew by tearing open her tiny bag of airline peanuts and chewing each one a dozen times so her mouth would stay busy.

Her mouth had gotten her into trouble so many times, she couldn't begin to count them all. When would she ever learn to keep quiet? Why couldn't she and Paul have talked about normal things like the weather? Why did she always have to speak her mind and be so intense, even with strangers?

That's what bothered her the most. Paul didn't seem like a stranger. Somehow they connected. Even Paul had to admit that. There was something between them, and it was powerful.

The plane landed on time in Portland. Paul and Sierra had spent the last ten minutes talking about hiking. He recommended several of his favorite places in the area. It was a calm, friendly chat, like two strangers are supposed to have on an airplane. She expressed her condolences about his grandfather, and he thanked her politely.

When they deplaned, Paul walked down the hallway beside her, as if they were together. He didn't say anything. He was just there.

As soon as they entered the terminal, Sierra scanned

the greeters, trying to pick out Jalene before he went to her. She found her immediately. With jet black hair cut severely short, Jalene wore a long skirt and black boots. She looked normal enough. Kind of cute and fun-looking, except for a cat smile that curled up her lips. Paul seemed to hesitate for an instant before walking into her open arms.

Sierra kept moving with the crowd, walking toward the baggage claim where she had arranged to meet her parents. On impulse she turned and looked over her shoulder one last time. She expected to see Paul kissing Jalene. However, from the looks of it, Jalene was the one doing the kissing.

Sierra stepped on the escalator and tried to shake thoughts of Paul from her mind. She had enough to deal with, including adjusting to the new house and a new school next week.

I don't even know his last name. I'm never going to see him again. It was nothing more than a strange encounter with an even stranger guy. I opened my mouth way too much, as usual. End of story.

Sierra spotted her dad the minute she stepped off the escalator. His eyes were all crinkled up in the kind of smile he wore when he was trying not to cry. Her mom stood beside him, looking slimmer than Sierra remembered. She was a youthful-looking woman who jogged regularly. Her blond hair was in a short bob, and she had on the black pants and red oversized sweater Sierra had given her for Christmas.

Sierra hurried into their embrace. First Dad hugged her, with a big kiss on the cheek, and then Mom, whose tears smeared across Sierra's face.

"It's so good to have you home!" Dad said. He looked young too, except for his receding hairline. Where the brown wispy hairs had thinned on top, rows of faint worry lines ran all the way up his extended forehead.

"It's weird thinking of Portland as home," Sierra said. She and her mom looped arms and walked over to where the other passengers were forming a line around the long luggage conveyor belt.

"I think you'll like it here," Mom said. "Granna Mae has been doing better since we arrived."

"Are we all moved in?" Sierra asked.

"Pretty much. A bunch of boxes are in the basement full of my knickknacks and books and things. There's not room for them on the shelves yet. Granna Mae and I need to do some sorting and cleaning. She's been asking for four days straight when you're coming home. Time is still a problem for her. Days and years all sort of blend together, and she has a hard time remembering where she is. Don't be surprised if she is confused when she sees you and can't quite place who you are."

"She'll know me," Sierra said confidently. "I'm glad she's feeling better."

A loud buzzer sounded, and the luggage conveyor belt began its cycle. Sierra stepped deeper into the crowd of travelers and stretched to see if her suitcase was coming yet. She spotted it and was about to reach for it when someone stepped in front of her and grabbed it.

"Hey, that's my bag!"

"No, it's mine," the guy said. He turned to face her. It was Paul.

chapter seven

"**I** DON'T BELIEVE THIS," PAUL SAID. "Your bag must look like mine, but this is my bag."

"Sorry, it's mine. Check the luggage tag."

He did, and it was hers.

"My mistake," Paul said, putting the bag down in the midst of all the people crammed around the conveyor belt.

"Yeah, well try not to make any more," Sierra said, deliberately looking beyond Paul to Jalene, who was waiting for him in the background.

A smile slipped onto Paul's face. He tilted back his hat so it hung by the strings around his neck. "I hope I never see you again," he said. "You're making my life very complicated."

Sierra thought of about four sharp comments she could make back to him, but she held her tongue. She wasn't sure why. Perhaps because all the bold comments on the plane had seemed so futile. Or maybe because her parents were standing only a few yards away, not to mention Jalene watching them.

Sierra said nothing but stood her ground and stared into his blue-gray eyes the way he had stared at her more than once. Paul stared right back. Their thirty-second stare-out felt as if it lasted an eternity. Sierra was the one who blinked first.

"Have a nice life," she said and walked away.

"Hey!" Paul called out after her. She ignored him and kept walking.

"You forgot your bag."

Sierra turned around. Paul was about two feet away from her, emerging from the crowd with her luggage.

Paul handed her the heavy travel bag, and without making eye contact this time, he said in a low voice, "Don't ever change, Sierra." Looking up at her for just an instant, he smiled, then turned, and headed back into the mob of people.

To her, this was the final truce. To the average observer she was sure the exchange seemed to be nothing more than a stranger helping someone to locate her luggage.

However, Sierra's dad didn't happen to be an average observer. After they arrived home and Sierra had been thoroughly hugged and welcomed by her two younger brothers, her dad invited her to sit out on the front porch with him. Granna Mae was already asleep, having apparently forgotten that Sierra was coming home tonight, and Tawni hadn't returned yet from her job at the Clackamas Town Center Mall.

Sierra made herself a cup of hot peppermint tea and

grabbed a thick lap comforter from the front hall closet. The screen on the front door squeaked as it had every summer that Sierra had come here since she was a baby.

Only now it was winter, and the wide, wraparound front porch was a chilly place to sit. Her dad was waiting for her on the swing. She sat next to him, balancing her tea and pulling the comforter over her legs.

"We all missed you, Sierra. It's good that you're home." She could see his breath as he spoke to her.

"Do you want some of my tea?" Sierra offered the steaming cup, and he took a sip.

He made a face. "What is that?"

"Peppermint."

"I think I'll stick to coffee." He liked it dark and thick, a tradition in his Danish family but one Sierra was unable to bring herself to participate in. On the few occasions she did have coffee, she tempered it with lots of cream and sugar. Artificially flavored creamers were even better. For the most part, Sierra was an herbal tea drinker.

"What was his name?" her father said.

"Who?"

"The young explorer with the hat who couldn't take his eyes off you." Sierra's dad rested his arm across the back of the porch swing, inviting Sierra to draw closer to him and share her thoughts.

She knew better than to beat around any bushes with her dad. When it came to his six children, Howard Jensen knew each of them by heart. Sierra did her best to reconstruct the unusual encounter with Paul and even told her dad about her impression to fight for Paul.

He rubbed his chin after she finished. The worry lines on his forehead began to smooth away. "That is what you must do then," he concluded.

"I don't even know his last name," Sierra said.

"God does. All you must do is pray for him. I'll pray with you. Every day. Now tell me about the rest of your trip."

"I don't know where to start. It was the most incredible experience of my life. I'm so glad I went." Sierra put down her empty mug and slipped her cold hands under the comforter. She began with a day-by-day rundown, when her mom joined them with two mugs of coffee. She handed one to Dad. Mom had on a long coat and her favorite Mukluk slippers. She curled up in a white wicker chair across from the swing. Sierra's dad wore only a sweater and pants yet he seemed warm enough. He loved the cold. Must be his Scandinavian blood.

"Oh, good," Sierra's mom said, sipping her rich coffee. "I didn't want to miss anything. I tucked in the boys and told them to let you sleep tomorrow, even if you end up sleeping all day."

"Thanks," Sierra said. "I probably could sleep all day. I don't even know if it's daytime or nighttime, according to my body."

Just then a teal-colored sedan pulled up and parked

in front of the house. Sierra's sister, Tawni, stepped out and pushed a button on her key chain, which made a melodic tone as it locked the car doors.

"Did Tawni get a new car?"

"Last week," Mom said. "Isn't it a beauty?"

Stately Tawni, with her model-like figure, sauntered up the five wide steps that led to the porch. A sweet fragrance preceded her, the aftereffect of her job at a perfume counter at Nordstrom. "You're home!" she said when she noticed Sierra. "Did you have a good time?"

Sierra slid off the swing and went over to hug Tawni since Tawni didn't seem to be moving toward Sierra. "It was fantastic! You should go next time." Sierra couldn't quite imagine Tawni traveling unless she was guaranteed a hot shower every morning and a place to plug in her curling iron. "I like your new car," Sierra said.

"Thanks." Tawni warmly reciprocated the hug. That's how Tawni was. She wouldn't initiate any sign of affection, but she responded sincerely when Sierra did.

Tawni was a beautiful woman and looked older than eighteen. Her appearance was enhanced by her expert use of makeup, her highlighted blond hair, and her tinted blue contacts. She had worn braces for three years and had had singing lessons since she was ten. In many ways, she and Sierra were opposites. They were congenial because they were related. Under other circumstances, they probably wouldn't have sought each other's friendship.

"I'm so broke now you wouldn't believe it," Tawni said. "This job at Nordstrom opened up just in time. I'm only scheduled for twenty-five hours a week to start, but it should turn into full-time by the first of March."

"That's great," Sierra said. "You want to grab a blanket and join us out here?"

"If you don't mind, I'm really tired. I'll hear all about your trip tomorrow. Did you see our room yet? At least it's bigger than the one we had in Pineville."

"The boys showed it to me right away. I take it my bed is the one by the window?"

"You don't mind, do you?" Tawni said. Sierra knew that since Tawni was already settled, it wouldn't matter if she did mind.

"No, it's fine. It's a great room. It's just weird to come home and have everything all turned around and you guys all settled and living here without me."

"Well, welcome home," Tawni said, moving toward the front door. "I'm going to bed."

"Good night, honey," their dad said.

"Sweet dreams," said Mom.

Sierra called out, "I'll try to be quiet when I go to bed."

Tawni went inside, and Sierra thought again, as she had hundreds, if not thousands of times, that she wished she could find a way to change her sister. Tawni seemed to carry a big chip on her shoulder because she was the only one of the six Jensen children who was adopted. Obviously she was wanted. She was always treated equally by Mom and Dad, and Sierra thought of Tawni as her one and only sister. But Tawni had labeled herself years ago and moved about their family with slight alienation.

"I didn't even ask you guys how you like it here," Sierra said, snuggling back under her comforter.

"It's home," Dad said.

"Well, of course it is to you, Dad. You grew up here. How are you doing, Mom? And the boys?"

"Actually, things are going better than I'd expected. Granna Mae has some good days when she's bright as a berry, but then other days her memory lapses, and she doesn't know who we are. This morning she asked Howard if he were here to fix the plumbing."

"Doesn't it kill you that your own mother doesn't know who you are?" Sierra asked.

"It's not her fault. I told her yes, I was the best plumber in all of Portland, and where was the leaky pipe. She led me right to the wash basin in the basement and told me how it was stopped up because a yo-yo was caught in it."

"That really happened," Mom told Sierra. "When your dad was about seven, he stuck his yo-yo in that sink, and they had to call a plumber to remove it so the rest of the drains wouldn't stop up. It was an expensive visit from the plumber, and Granna Mae talked about it for years."

"So now she's remembering things that happened in the past and sort of acting them out?" Sierra asked.

"Something like that," Dad answered.

"It's going to be hard for me to be around her when she's spacing out like that," Sierra said. "She was perfectly fine last summer. What happened? Can't they give her something? Some medicine or some kind of treatment?"

Mom shook her head. "We just have to keep an eye on her. It seems best to play along whenever she's having one of her memory lapses. It upsets her when we try to tell her who we really are or force her back into the present."

Sierra and her parents talked for almost an hour before it became too cold and Sierra was yawning so much that she couldn't complete her sentences. She hugged her mom and dad and climbed the curved staircase up to her new room.

Tawni had left on a small light on the bed stand between their twin beds. It cast a soft yellow glow on the striped rose wallpaper and the white wooden shutters lining the bottom half of the bedroom window.

This room had belonged to Aunt Emma, Dad's baby sister. When Emma moved out many years ago, it had become a catchall room since it was so large. For every summer that Sierra could remember, coming into this room was like exploring an old attic. With all the old clutter cleared out and the room now cleaned up and filled with Sierra's and Tawni's familiar belongings, it had turned into a wonderful bedroom.

Sierra noticed it was especially cold by the window.

She made sure the shutters that covered the old glass panes were completely shut, blocking out the night draft. Her feet were still cold from sitting on the porch. It would feel good to slide in between those flannel sheets.

But before Sierra climbed into bed, she felt she should do something to christen her new room. It had to be something quiet so she wouldn't wake Tawni.

Sierra decided to pray. She knelt beside her bed, with the chilly window to her back and with her hands folded and eyes closed. She prayed silently for Granna Mae, her family, herself, and her friends from Carnforth Hall. Then she prayed for Paul.

When Sierra opened her eyes, a scream caught in her throat. Someone was sitting on her bed. The silent figure wore a white gown and a glow came from around its head. Sierra could feel her heart pounding as the figure rose and pulled back the covers for Sierra. It moved away from the light and spoke to her. "Did you remember to pray for Paul, Emma dear?"

"Granna Mae," Sierra whispered. The confused woman stood in her flannel nightgown, her white hair all fuzzy around her head, waiting for Sierra to climb into bed. Sierra remembered what her mom had said about playing along so she obediently crawled into bed.

Why did she ask if I prayed for Paul? Does she know about the guy on the plane? Why does she think I'm Emma? Because I'm in Emma's room?

Granna Mae had a peaceful smile on her face as she tucked the covers in all around Sierra and kissed her on both cheeks as if she were a little girl who had just said her prayers.

"Repeat after me, Emma dear: 'The Lord thy God in the midst of thee is mighty.'"

Sierra hesitated.

"Go ahead, Emma dear. 'The Lord thy God . . .'"

"'The Lord thy God in the midst of thee is mighty.'" Sierra repeated in a small voice. Her heart was still pounding.

"'He will save, He will rejoice over thee with joy; He will rest in His love,'" Granna Mae said tenderly.

Sierra repeated it.

"'He will joy over thee with singing.'"

Again Sierra repeated, "'He will joy over thee with singing.'"

"Amen," said Granna Mae.

"Amen," Sierra echoed.

Then, as silently as she had appeared in the bedroom, Granna Mae shuffled out in her bare feet, shutting the door behind her.

chapter eight

"MOTHER, YOU CAN'T TELL ME THAT'S normal," Sierra argued in a hushed voice the next morning in the kitchen.

"For her, for right now, it is normal. We all have to be understanding. That's what we agreed to when we came here, Sierra." Mom turned off the whistling tea kettle, and the stove's black knob came off in her hand. She held it up in front of Sierra and said, "And this is the other reason! This old house is falling apart. It's not safe for her to be here alone."

"But is it safe for us to be here with her?"

"Of course it is! Her mind is playing tricks on her, that's all. You did the right thing last night by playing along and letting her think she was tucking Emma into bed. That was probably a very soothing and warm memory for her."

"But why did she ask if I prayed for Paul?"

"I'm sure she meant her son Paul. Did you remember that Dad had a brother who was killed in Vietnam?"

"I didn't even think of him," Sierra said, pouring the

hot water into a bowl of instant oatmeal. "It's too spooky for me, Mom. I felt as if I should sleep with one eye open just in case she came back in the middle of the night."

"Try to imagine what it must be like for her," Mom said. "Treat her with dignity."

"I'll try." She poured some milk into her oatmeal, stirred it around, and lifted the spoon to her mouth. Just then, Granna Mae stepped into the kitchen.

"Well, look who's here!" she said. Sierra wasn't sure if Granna Mae thought she was looking at Sierra, Emma, or maybe even someone else, like the plumber.

"Good morning," Sierra said with a smile. She slowly pushed the stool away from the kitchen counter and stood before Granna Mae, waiting for her cue as to whom Sierra should be for her grandma this morning.

"Well? Don't you have a little hug for me, Lovey?"

Sierra knew her grandmother recognized her when she said "Lovey." She had pet names for all her grand-kids, and that was Sierra's. With a sigh of relief, Sierra met her grandma's hug and even gave her a kiss on the cheek. Granna Mae smelled like soap, all clean and fresh.

"Don't let me interrupt your breakfast," she said. She stepped lightly to the cupboard, pulled out a china teacup, and poured herself some of the strong, black coffee warming in the Braun coffeemaker on the counter. She always drank from a china cup, even water with her daily pills. Perish the thought that she would ever lift anything plastic or, horrors, Styrofoam to her lips. It was a china cup or nothing. Sierra remembered going on family picnics as a child and, wrapped in a cloth napkin at the bottom of the picnic hamper, would be Granna Mae's favorite china teacup.

"I'd love to hear all about your trip, Lovey. I was simply too tired last night to wait up for you. I hope you understand."

"Of course," Sierra said. "My trip was wonderful. I loved Ireland, and I made a lot of great friends." For the next twenty minutes or so Sierra chatted about her trip. Granna Mae sat on the cushioned bench along the back kitchen wall and listened with clear-eyed interest. Sierra found it hard to believe this was the same person who had done the angel imitation in Sierra's bedroom last night.

During the next three days, Granna Mae seemed normal, spunky, quick-witted, and hardworking. Sierra loved being around her. They talked lots and laughed about silly things. They worked together helping Mom clear off the bookshelves in the downstairs library. Most of the photos and mementos were moved up to Granna Mae's room, where Sierra's dad had built new shelves along one entire wall. Granna Mae seemed pleased to have all her things near her.

Sierra was impressed that her grandma was so willing to share her well-established home with Sierra's family. After living in the same house for forty-two of her sixty-eight years, she was gracious about letting

Sierra's mom come in and rearrange everything. Mom had even ordered new furniture for the family room, including a couch that folded out to a queen sleeper. Granna Mae's little television with the rabbit ears antennae was sent up to her room, where she had better reception than she had ever gotten downstairs.

The TV corner was now empty, which made the family room look lopsided with all the new furniture in place. Dad was building an entertainment center out in the cottage behind the house that he had turned into his workroom. It was actually an old playhouse with tacky gingerbread trim around the roof and windows. But nothing was childish about what went on inside it now that Dad had set up his workbench and lined the wall with Peg-Board and all his power tools. Dillon and Gavin loved going out there and with their own hammers and saws creating "masterpieces." Granna Mae referred to it as "the boys' clubhouse."

Then, the night before Sierra started school, Granna Mae had one of her relapses at dinner. They were sitting around the mahogany table in the formal dining room when all of a sudden Granna Mae turned to Gavin and said, "You cannot leave this table until you eat your peas, young man." She stood up and cleared her place, taking her still full dinner plate into the kitchen.

Six-year-old, freckle-faced Gavin looked at his mom with distress. "We're not even having peas," he said.

"I know, honey. She's confused. It's okay."

Granna Mae returned a few moments later wearing a mitt pot holder on her hand and carrying in an apple pie. In her other hand she held a knife. She had a smile on her face. "Now I told Ted we would save him a piece of this pie. You children mind that you don't take too much for yourselves." She set down the pie on the table. "I suppose I should cut it for you so it will be fair. This is the only pie we have, and it must go around." She pressed the knife into the center of the pie, but nothing happened. "Oh, me. I brought the wrong knife." Granna Mae drifted back into the kitchen.

"It's frozen," Sierra said.

"I know. I put it out on the counter to let it thaw," Mom said. "I planned on putting it in the oven after dinner."

"Mom," Dillon said, "is it safe for her to be walking around with knives like that?" Dillon was eight and looked like Sierra's dad only with more hair. Dillon was the serious, responsible child, who seemed to believe his mission in life was to make sure his fearless younger brother, Gavin, lived to be a teenager. Dillon had caught Gavin playing Ninja warrior with Mom's chef knife about three years ago. When he wrestled the knife away from Gavin, Dillon received a minor cut on the palm of his hand. His concern for Granna Mae was sincere.

"We'll keep a close eye on her," Mom said. She looked to Dad for support.

"I better go check on her," Dad said and strode into

the kitchen. It was quiet as they all waited, eating and listening.

Dad finally returned with Granna Mae beside him. "It was a fine dinner," he was saying to her.

"Did the children save you enough pie?"

"Yes, yes they did. You go on up to bed now. I'll have the children do the dishes for you."

"If you're sure you don't mind," Granna Mae said, heading for the hallway that led to the stairs.

"Not at all. You get some sleep now."

Granna Mae shuffled off down the hallway, and Dad returned to the table. He seemed upset.

"Is she okay?" Dillon asked.

Dad nodded and silently stuck his fork into his now cold mashed potatoes. "She was doing so well the past few days. I didn't expect her to switch on us so quickly."

"What was she doing?" Gavin asked.

"She thought we were her children, and she was serving dinner like she always did. She's gone to bed now. She'll be fine."

Sierra watched her mom give Dad a look that said, "How can you be sure she'll be fine?"

The situation with Granna Mae tore at Sierra that night as she tried to sleep. Her body still had nights and days mixed up, and she was fighting off feelings of uncertainty about starting school the next morning. All this emotional energy focused on Granna Mae. Sixty-eight wasn't old for a grandmother. Her body was strong and healthy. It seemed cruel and unfair that her mind would fail her when her body had so many more healthy years left.

Sierra's Grandpa Ted had died when Sierra was little. She only had a vague memory of the funeral and wasn't sure what had caused his death. He had been a builder for thirty-some years, as his father had been for many years before him. Sierra's great-grandfather built this house in 1915, which was partly why Granna Mae couldn't bring herself to sell it. Sierra knew her father was too compassionate to ever send his mother to a rest home. So here they were, adjusting to a new life in a new city with a grandmother who was slowly going crazy.

Tawni entered the bedroom quietly while Sierra was deep in her disturbing thoughts. A distinct sweet fragrance entered with her. "You don't have to tiptoe, Tawni. I'm still awake."

"Do you mind if I turn on the light?" As she asked the question she turned it on.

Sierra pulled up the blanket to cover her eyes. "How was work?"

"Fine."

"Granna Mae flipped out a little at dinner. She thought we were all her children."

"You should have seen her the day we moved in," Tawni said. "She acted as if we were all workers who had come to repair her house. I wish they could do something for her."

"I know. Doesn't it kind of scare you to think about

getting old and losing your mind like that?" Sierra
asked.

"I don't know." Tawni slipped off her shoes and sat
on the edge of her bed. "It's probably hereditary. You
have her genes; I don't. At least you know. Who knows
what hereditary diseases I'm carrying around."

Sierra had heard Tawni talk like this before. It was
sort of a martyr thing. At the same time, what she said
was true. She didn't know the medical history of her
birth family. Sierra would probably feel the same way
if she were in Tawni's position.

"But I intend to find out," Tawni said, scooping up
her shoes and walking over to the closet. Tawni's side of
the closet was perfect. Everything had a proper place,
and that's how she kept it. All the time.

Sierra had a much more liberal system for keeping
track of her things. If it was in the way, move it. If you
can't find it, wear something else.

Tawni's comment sank in. Sierra raised herself on
one elbow and squinted at the light. "What do you
mean you intend to find out?"

"I'm going to find my birth mother," Tawni said,
without turning around. "As soon as I save enough
money."

"Why do you want to do that?"

Tawni spun around, looking surprised and almost
hurt that Sierra would even have to ask.

"Never mind," Tawni said. "You wouldn't understand."

chapter nine

MONDAY MORNING MOM DROVE SIERRA ten miles across town to Royal Christian Academy. It was raining, as usual, and Sierra shivered in the front seat of their old VW Rabbit, waiting for the heater to kick in. She looked at her blue knit shirt, her long patchwork skirt, and her cowboy boots. She touched her earrings again, trying to remember which ones she had put on.

For one of the first times in her life she felt self-conscious about her clothes. Being an individual in Pineville had been cool. Her high school was small, and she was popular, especially because all the teachers had liked her two brothers and sister who had gone before her.

Now she was starting her first day at a private Christian school, and she imagined all 279 of the other students were a bunch of clones, wearing navy blue outfits with white socks.

"Mom," Sierra said, as they sped down the freeway, "I'm beginning to think this Christian school idea isn't the way for me to go. I've always been in public school, except when you home-schooled me. I don't think I'll like it. It's just not *me*."

Sierra's mom was generally a patient counselor. Sierra felt she could come to her anytime and talk to her about anything. This morning was different. Mom seemed on edge.

"We've been through this," she said sharply. "When we made the decision to move here, we talked with you about it, and you decided you would like to go to the Christian high school since you never had that opportunity in Pineville."

"I know," Sierra said. "But that was before I went to Europe. I don't think I'm going to have anything in common with any of the people at this school. I'm just not like them."

"And how do you know all this without having even seen the school or met a single student, hmmm?" Mom turned the windshield wipers on full speed. "It's not like you, Sierra, to be afraid of the unknown like this. What happened to your adventuresome spirit?"

"I don't know."

"Give it a try," Mom said, pulling off the freeway and driving four blocks to the high school. "One week is all I ask. Then we'll have this conversation again. Okay?" She stopped the car in front of the two main doors.

Sierra hesitated. It looked like a normal school. She spotted a few students entering the building who had on normal-looking clothes, nothing uniform-like or old-fashioned.

"One week," Sierra said.

"Do you want me to come into the office with you?" Mom asked.

"No, I'm fine." Sierra pulled her backpack over her shoulder and opened the door.

"I'll pick you up at 3:15," Mom said, leaning across the seat. "Have a good day, honey!"

Sierra forced a smile. The office was easy to find, and as soon as she walked in, a frizzy-haired woman with glasses said, "You must be Sierra Jensen. Welcome to Royal!" Sierra didn't smile back.

"Here's your class schedule and some other papers for you to look at, including our handbook."

I knew it! Here come all the rules.

The secretary began to run through a list of information such as where her locker was, what time they broke for lunch, how she could still sign up for the girls' basketball team (if she were interested), and how chapel was on Fridays. Most of the information bounced off of Sierra.

"Randy should be here any minute," the lady said. "I asked him to show you around." She glanced at the large, round clock on the side wall. "Well, where is he? You only have ten minutes before the bell rings."

"I'm sure I can find everything on my own. Thanks."

"Don't be ridiculous. This is a big school, and we don't want you getting lost on your first day."

Sierra felt like telling the woman that last week she had managed to get herself from the Lake District of England all the way to Heathrow Airport and then to

Portland. Certainly she could find locker number 117 without a Seeing Eye dog.

Just then a tall guy with longish hair walked into the office. Sierra was surprised. She would have expected a rule about hair length in the handbook. It wasn't that his hair was terribly long. It was dirty blond, combed straight back, and hanging about an inch below his ears. His clothes were also a surprise. He had on a bronze-colored jacket with a fur-lined hood. If Sierra had found such a jacket on one of her thrift store excursions, she would have felt she had bagged a treasure, no matter what the price.

"Hey, new girl!" Randy said.

"Her name is Sierra," the secretary said. "Now show her around quickly before classes start."

Randy stuck out his arm as if he were supposed to escort her down the aisle at a wedding. Sierra motioned that both her hands were full with all the papers.

"Whatever," Randy said and walked out into the hallway, which was now beginning to thicken with students. "Cool boots," he said.

"I like your jacket," Sierra said.

"My dad bought it in Nepal. Now, your locker is right here. Did they give you the combination?"

Sierra was delighted that at least one person in this school was related to someone who had been outside the U.S. She found the paper with the combination on it and spun the numbers around. It opened right away, and a dozen purple and gold balloons tumbled out.

"That's our traditional welcome," Randy said. "Now you're official or whatever."

Sierra didn't know what to think. People were walking past them, looking but not stopping. She still had her arms full, and yet she had to try to collect all the balloons and figure out what to do with them. Randy just stood there watching. Still, it was a nice surprise, something she would never have experienced at Pineville High.

"We can pop 'em," Randy said, pinching the latex on one balloon and biting into it so that the air came hissing out. He popped a few more while Sierra tried to cram the rest back into her locker. She didn't have any books so nothing else needed to fit into her locker yet.

Once she shut the locker door, Randy said, "Come on. I'll show you where the classrooms are. What do you have first period?"

Sierra followed him down the hall and scanned the papers in her hand. "If this is it, then I have English first."

"Cool," Randy said. "So do I. It's right here." He pointed to a door on the left but kept walking. "Down that hall is the gym. For P.E. you go into the door on the right at the very end." He kept walking. "Now that hall," he said, motioning to the left, "is the lowlife ward. It leads to the junior high wing. You don't ever want to get lost and wander off down there!"

A bell rang above their heads. Randy turned around and started to walk back the way they had come. "I'll

look for you at lunch," he said. "Did I show you where
the cafeteria is?"

"No. But don't worry. I'm sure I can find it."

They were back at the door to their English class.
Randy stopped by the door and let Sierra enter first. He
followed her in and said in a loud voice, "This is Sierra,
everybody." Then to her in a lower voice he said, "You
can sit wherever you want."

Sierra slid into the closest desk, aware that everyone
was looking at her. Somehow all this friendly-welcome
stuff bugged her. She was sure the administration
meant well, sending Randy to show her around and
filling her locker with balloons, but it made her uncom-
fortable. She felt too welcomed. She had expected a
school of stuck-up students all ignoring her. That would
have made it easy for her to slip in and out unnoticed.
It also would have made it easier for her to leave after
a week and never be missed.

"Look!" said a dark-haired girl, wearing a patchwork
jumper with a turtleneck underneath. "We match."

Sierra had not expected that. Her clothes *never*
matched anyone else's. Ever.

"Did you get yours at A Wrinkle in Time?" the girl
asked. She had dark, expressive eyes and olive-toned
skin. "That's my favorite vintage store in Hawthorne."

"I've never been there," Sierra said. And then, because
it came out so abruptly, she added, "My skirt came
from a thrift store in Sacramento."

"Is that where you're from?" the girl asked.

"No." Sierra didn't offer any further explanation because the teacher was starting the class and everyone was seated except the girl in the matching patchwork dress.

The teacher briefly welcomed Sierra, who felt relieved a big deal wasn't made over her. The class time was mostly lecture and not discussion, which was good. She could melt into the background a little more easily.

Melting in turned out to be Sierra's goal for the day. She remained quiet and reserved in each class. At lunch she sat with Randy and some of his friends because he made such a fuss about it when she walked into the cafeteria. But when she answered their initial questions with only a simple "yes" or "no," they all turned their attention to other topics and closed her out. And that's what she wanted.

"Lovey?" Granna Mae called from the kitchen when Sierra and her mom walked in after school. "I'm all ready to go. Will you drive me to Eaton's?"

Sierra looked to her mom for an explanation. Mom only shrugged her shoulders. Sierra thought her grandmother was dealing in the present, since she had used the term "Lovey." But what was this plan of hers to go to Eaton's Drug Store?

"Do you need to pick up a prescription, Granna Mae?" Sierra asked.

"No." She buttoned the big black buttons on her red coat and pulled the black fur collar up around her neck. Then, adjusting a black mohair tam on her head, she moved toward the door. Granna Mae looked cute, like a little girl on her way to a Christmas party.

"I guess we'll be back in a little while," Sierra said, dropping her backpack by the front hall tree and scooping up the keys to the Rabbit from off the entry table. With Granna Mae's arm looped through hers, they took the wet steps down the front porch slowly.

Sierra drove the six blocks to the pharmacy carefully. The roads were slick, plus this was the first time she had driven a car in more than a month. It felt funny to be behind the wheel, especially in an area she had never driven in before.

During her summer visits to Granna Mae's, she and her brothers and sister had walked to Eaton's many times on the warm afternoons. Inside an original fountain and grill with a long formica counter and red vinyl stools waited for them. Sierra had consumed many ice cream cones and root beer floats at that counter. It was one of the few businesses in the area that had remained operative since the first day it opened, more than fifty years ago. Some of the other older businesses along the same street had been torn down or renovated and turned into gift shops or espresso stands.

Granna Mae hummed contentedly as they pulled into the small parking lot and maneuvered through the puddles to the back door. A bell rang as they entered, and Sierra was flooded with memories of the place.

"What do you need today, Granna Mae?" asked Sierra, automatically heading for the pharmaceutical counter.

Granna Mae headed in the other direction, toward the fountain. Sierra followed her and sat down on a stool next to her grandmother, still a little confused as to what was going on.

"Mae, how are you doing today?" the woman behind the counter in the white apron asked. Sierra recognized her. She had been working there ever since Sierra had first come in.

"Very well. Did you notice Howard's daughter here with me, Angie?" Granna Mae asked, removing her coat and hat and draping them over the vacant stool next to her.

"Why, is that little Sierra? My, how you've grown, honey! I heard you had a rather exciting trip to the Emerald Isle. Did you find it to your liking?"

"Yes, thank you. It was a great trip. I'd love to go back again one day."

"I imagine you will," the sweet woman said. "Mae always said you had the spark for a lark. Now, what can I get you ladies today?"

"We need the usual first-day-of-school treat with two glasses. And I'd like a cup of coffee too. Anything else for you, Lovey?"

Since Sierra wasn't exactly sure what the "usual" was, she ordered a glass of water.

Granna Mae's soft face turned up in a smile as she transferred her attention from Angie to Sierra. "Did your father ever tell you how I used to do this with all the children? On the first day of school we walked over here to Eaton's and ordered chocolate malts. It used to be the little ones couldn't wait for their first day of school just so they would have their chance to come. I haven't done this since Emma was in grade school."

Angie set the glass of water and cup of coffee in front of them. Granna Mae went to work, preparing her coffee. First, just the right amount of cream was poured in from the silver-colored creamer Angie slid across the counter to them. Then precisely half of a packet of sugar, torn open only at the corner, was added.

Sierra enjoyed Granna Mae's hands. They were dancing hands. Each movement of her fingers seemed liquid and smoothly connected to the next movement. She lifted her spoon as if it were a feather and created a whirlpool within the white ceramic mug. Apparently Eaton's coffee mugs were an acceptable substitute for a china cup.

"One year," Granna Mae said, picking up her thought, "we had seven Jensen children and myself lined up on the first day of school. We nearly took up the whole counter!"

Sierra knew that Granna Mae had always been careful with her money. She was surprised that her grandma would spend money on seven chocolate malts simply to celebrate the first day of school.

"Now tell me about your first day, Lovey."

Sierra shrugged. "There's not much to tell."

"That's not an answer. Tell me about everything. I want to hear it all."

"Well, it's different from Pineville in a lot of ways, especially when my English teacher started the class with a Bible verse and prayer. That was a nice change from public school."

"Indeed it was! And that's how things should be in school."

Angie placed two fluted glasses in front of them, filled with the rich chocolate malt. She also gave them the metal canister she had used to blend the ice cream.

Granna Mae chuckled. "And to think I used to be able to finish off one of these by myself!"

Sierra stuck her straw into the glass and savored the treat. "Thanks, Granna Mae. This is really nice of you. I appreciate it."

"It's my delight, Lovey. Now tell me more about your school."

Sierra tried to think of things to say. Inwardly she was still planning to finish out the week and then tell her parents she wanted to enroll in the public high school. She told Granna Mae about the balloons in her locker and how she popped them all and threw them away at the end of the day so she could stick her books inside.

"Oh, and then, if you can believe this," Sierra said, "a girl in three of my classes had a dress on that was made out of the same material as my skirt. The chances of that happening are pretty rare, don't you think?"

"You should go shopping with her then. She has your taste."

The comment felt abrasive to Sierra. Nobody had her taste. Her clothes were her trademark. That wasn't something she shared.

"As a matter of fact, why don't you invite her over sometime? What's her name?"

"I don't know."

Granna Mae looked at Sierra with a hint of disappointment pulling down her sometimes droopy right eye. She didn't say anything, but her hands danced to her coffee mug. She lifted it and sipped slowly.

Sierra felt the need to redirect the conversation. "Do you remember that one girl I told you about from Carnforth? Katie? I invited her to visit me sometime. She might come up this summer. You'll like her; she's a lot of fun."

"Did you learn the names of any of the other students today?" Granna Mae didn't fall for the diversion.

"Yes."

"And what are their names?"

"Well, I met a guy named Randy. He had a really nice coat. He said it was from Nepal."

"And?" Granna Mae prodded.

"And his father bought it for him." Sierra knew that wasn't the trail of conversation Granna Mae had been trying to direct her down. She couldn't help it. All this questioning made her feel guilty, even though Granna Mae hadn't said anything that should make her feel scolded.

Angie stepped back over to fill Granna Mae's coffee

mug. She made friendly conversation with Granna Mae, which Sierra was glad for. It meant she didn't have to give any more answers about school. It had been hard enough finding satisfactory answers for her mom on the way home from school.

Granna Mae took her time on her malt and coffee. An elderly man came in and sat a few seats down. He and Granna Mae greeted each other and asked the customary questions. The man seemed to know who Sierra was, even though she couldn't remember if he was a neighbor or what. His presence added a further opportunity for sidetracking Granna Mae from her mission to probe into Sierra's first day of school.

When they left, Granna Mae paid the check and left a quarter for a tip. Sierra thought that was awfully chintzy. She wished she had some money on her so she could leave more.

As they stepped outside, they found the sun had broken through the clouds, making rainbows in the oily puddles in the asphalt.

"Thanks again for the treat," Sierra said as they drove through a maze of old houses in the Mt. Tabor district of Portland. She could see why Granna Mae had put down her foot about moving out of this area. Besides being a beautiful neighborhood, she also had lifelong friends and neighbors. She was connected. And in a very real way, Sierra envied her.

chapter ten

*T*HE SECOND DAY OF SCHOOL SIERRA continued her role as the uninterested observer. Nothing anybody said or did received much of a response from her until she was at her locker after school. She had just closed the metal locker door and turned around, when right in front of her was a brown leather backpack on the back of a guy. She had seen that backpack before. It was like Paul's.

Sierra hurried down the hall so she could pass the guy and then nonchalantly turn around and look at him. She knew it wasn't Paul. No way. What would he be doing there? Still, she had to look.

When she was about five feet in front of him, Sierra turned her head and looked at the backpack's wearer. She recognized him as the guy who sat in front of her in biology. He caught her glance and gave her a shy smile.

Oh, great! Now he thinks I'm trying to get his attention.

He wasn't an ugly guy or anything, sort of average in every way—average height, average brown hair, average facial features. He looked like the kind of guy whose favorite ice cream flavor was vanilla. Not at all the sort of person she was drawn toward. He was probably nothing like Paul.

For a moment Sierra was bothered that she had used Paul as a standard by which to judge other guys. How could she compare them? She didn't even know Paul. She would never see him again. Why should he even be in her thoughts?

Sierra kept walking down the hall and out the double doors until she spotted her mom in the car-pool line.

"So?" Mom asked as she maneuvered the little car out of the school parking lot. "Was today any better?"

"It was fine," Sierra said.

"I don't need the car tomorrow," Mom said. "You can drive, if you want to. If you need to stay after school for anything, that would be fine too."

Sierra knew what her mom was hinting at. She had brought up the topic of joining a school club at the dinner table the night before. Sierra had quickly used the excuse that all the clubs met after school. Now Mom was eliminating that obstacle.

"Sure," Sierra said, careful to avoid any suspicion, "I'll take the car tomorrow." The rest of the way home she paid careful attention so she could find her way back tomorrow.

She had no trouble finding her way *to* school on Wednesday. However, she met with difficulty getting back home. She left right after school was out and entered the freeway with no problem. Then she missed the off-ramp and ended up driving into thick traffic that led to downtown Portland. She didn't want to exit on the next off-ramp unless she was sure an on-ramp existed that would take her back the direction she had come. That way she would be sure to find her way home.

Sierra passed up the next two off-ramps. The first one didn't have a freeway return. The second one did, but she couldn't tell that until after she had already driven by. Before she realized it, she was approaching one of the huge bridges that crossed the Columbia River and that led to downtown Portland.

"Oh, man! What am I going to do?"

She felt dwarfed in her little car by all the vehicles passing her on either side. She drove slowly, trying to think through her next move. Just knowing water was underneath her gave her the heebie-jeebies. Nothing like this bridge existed in Pineville. And she had never driven in so much traffic.

Sierra curled up her toes inside her boots and quickly tried to think through her choices. She could find a phone, call her dad, and ask him to come rescue her. No. She could stop and ask someone how to get back to Granna Mae's house. At least she knew what district she lived in. That was a possibility. But the best scenario would be to find her own way back. If she could turn around and retrace her trail, she should be fine.

With renewed determination, Sierra clutched the

steering wheel and exited the bridge into the business district and a maze of one-way streets. As soon as she found a place to turn, Sierra made a right and followed the one-way street until she could make another right. She was headed for a freeway on-ramp.

"Okay, okay!" she hollered at the driver behind her who honked because she was going too slowly. She gave the car a little more gas and wished her parents would have acquired Oregon license plates. She could imagine the guy behind her yelling, "Californian, go home!" She refused to look at him in her rearview mirror. Besides, she had way too much ahead to concentrate on.

For example, which off-ramp to take. She drove quite a while before any exits appeared. The first one didn't sound familiar at all so she tried to switch lanes to avoid the off-ramp. But it was too late. The car behind her was on her tail, and a steady stream of cars was passing her on the left. She had no choice but to exit.

Sierra drove off to who knows where. But at times like these her adventuresome spirit kicked in, and she refused to be overcome. She drove a few blocks until she came to a gas station, parked to the side, and walked into the mini-mart connected to the gas station. Then, acting as if this were all planned, Sierra bought herself a Mars candy bar and a Portland map.

Just as Sierra was exiting the mini-mart, she saw a sports car pull in. The driver was Jalene; Sierra was sure of it. Jalene appeared to be alone. Wondering if Jalene would recognize her, Sierra considered talking to her.

As Sierra thought through her options, a black Jeep Wrangler bounced into the gas station, with its radio loudly playing music. Two college-age guys were in the Jeep. Sierra remembered seeing several older students in the mini-mart, and she realized she must be near Lewis and Clark. Now her options increased.

Sierra found herself smiling for the first time that day as she climbed back into her car and unfolded the Portland map.

Katie would probably call this a God-thing, my getting lost and ending up so close to Lewis and Clark. What if I drove around campus and had a look? Maybe God directed me here so I could bump into Paul.

She felt her heart beating faster as she located her position on the map and realized she was less than two blocks from the campus. Her parents wouldn't worry about her being late since Mom had encouraged her to stay after school. Still, she felt sneaky.

Should she call? That would be a good idea. Sierra fumbled in her backpack for some phone change and the slip of paper that had her new phone number on it. She couldn't believe she hadn't memorized it yet. Numbers just weren't her thing.

Locating the paper with the phone number, Sierra unfolded it and let out a groan. The paper must have gotten wet, because all the numbers were now smeared. She could dial several combinations of numbers until she came up with the right one. No good. She had less than a dollar in change after buying the map and candy bar. She could call information and ask. That would be good. Actually, that would be wise.

Sierra tore open the candy wrapper and took a nibble of her Mars bar. She remembered Cody once saying it was easier to say "I'm sorry" than "May I please." His philosophy certainly applied to this situation. If she did call home and say she was going to drive around the campus, her Mom would probably tell her to come home and they would go another time, together.

However, getting lost and ending up here wasn't something she had planned. It was really quite innocent. She could have a quick peek around campus and then, with the help of the map, find her way home. Her story would be as true as could be.

Chomping into the candy bar and chewing a big chunk now, Sierra decided to take the "I'm sorry" route. It wasn't as if she were disobeying or anything. This was one of those gray areas her dad had talked to her about, one of the many decisions a teen needs to make for herself and then be willing to live with the consequences of that choice. No problem. What kind of consequences could there be to a simple spin around some college campus?

A light rain began to fall as Sierra swallowed the last bite of her candy bar and backed her VW Rabbit out of the parking place at the gas station. She waited for an opening in the traffic before pulling onto the street. Glancing in her rearview mirror, she noticed Jalene's car was right behind her. She doubted that Jalene had even seen her, let alone recognized her as one of many passengers at the airport baggage claim a week ago.

When the first clearing appeared in the flow of traffic, Sierra pulled out and puttered the two blocks toward the university with Jalene right behind her. Sierra wished it were the other way around, and she was the one trailing Jalene. Who knows? Jalene might even lead her to Paul. Now that would be interesting.

Something inside Sierra didn't feel right. A subtle voice kept telling her that she had stepped a little too far outside the safety zone. At the same time, an urge within her pushed her forward, insisting she be daring. That rugged pioneer spirit of hers rose to the surface, and she forged ahead, entering the campus with Jalene right behind her.

Sierra kept an eye on Jalene's sports car as it turned into a parking lot beside a large building, which was about six stories high. One side of the building was glass windows. Sierra wondered what the impressive building was. She watched Jalene get out of her car and jog in the drizzle toward the building with some books under her arm. The library, maybe?

Sierra could venture into the library, couldn't she? She parked and swiftly darted into the building. It was the library. And it was full of college students. Sierra wondered what the chances were that Paul would be in the library right now. She didn't see Jalene anywhere.

Sierra walked past the front desk and past the card files on the left and stopped. All along the windows were sequestered nooks, each filled with students. What if Jalene had come to the library to meet Paul? What if they were sitting in one of those study areas right now, and Sierra happened to bump into them? What would she say, "Your girlfriend followed me over here, and now I'm following her"?

She glanced around one more time, impetuous enough to stay simply because she liked it here. She liked being around college students. This was where she felt she fit in, much more than at high school. These students and the campus had a maturity about them, and it suited her just fine. She saw herself as one of them.

"Excuse me," a male voice said softly.

Sierra spun around, expecting to see Paul and, at the same time, dreading it.

A bespectacled student who was shorter than Sierra stood next to her. He shifted the load of books under his arm and said, "You have a candy wrapper on your . . . well . . . back." His eyes moved to Sierra's behind.

She tried to turn to see what he meant. Somehow her Mars bar wrapper had gotten stuck to the seat of her jeans, and she had walked around the whole library that way.

"Oh, thank you," she said, peeling off the wrapper and appearing unruffled. A glob of chocolate and caramel remained on her jeans. Sierra took even, steady steps through the library, out the door, and straight to her car.

chapter eleven

W HAT SIERRA HAD NOT COUNTED ON was the heavy, after-work traffic. She had studied the map carefully and had found the freeway with no problem. The freeway, though, was more like a parking lot. Everyone in Portland seemed to want to go the direction she was going. The best she could do was inch along and flip through the radio stations, trying to find company for the commute home.

She located a Christian radio station, which was playing a song by one of her favorite performers, Margaret Becker. "Go, Margaret!" Sierra said as the singer hit a note square on and held it for all she was worth. Sierra sang along with her and sneaked another peek at her map.

She arrived home at ten after five. The minute she walked in the door, she knew she was in trouble.

"I got lost," she quickly pleaded before her mother had a chance to explode. "I ended up at Lewis and Clark somehow. I bought a map and found out how to get home, but the traffic was really heavy."

"Why didn't you call?" Mom said. Her arms were still folded across her chest, and her face was still red. It did seem she was a little relieved to hear Sierra's explanation.

"I thought about it, but I didn't have the number."

"Sierra," Mom said, shaking her head, "I'm not going to buy that one."

"Look," Sierra said, reaching into her backpack and pulling out the smeared phone number.

"You learned how to dial information long ago. The wet paper is no excuse. Now go wash up. Dinner is on the table."

This was the worst, going to dinner with an unresolved problem. It meant Sierra's situation would be discussed among the family members at the dinner table. She would rather have been yelled at by her mom or dad and gotten it over with.

The truth was, neither of them hardly ever yelled. Almost all their family problems were handled with discussions. Everyone was free to express his or her feelings and opinions at any time.

After her father prayed over the meal, he asked Sierra to explain again what had happened, which she did. This time she included the part about going into the library.

"Did you see him?" her father asked.

"No," Sierra said. *Does my dad know me, or what?*

"See who?" Gavin asked, his six-year-old curiosity piqued.

"A young man named Paul," Dad said.

"Paul?" Granna Mae asked. She sat motionless, and Sierra feared her grandmother's mind might do another one of its time warps. Then Granna Mae looked down at her plate and began to quietly eat her peas.

"I met him on the plane coming back from England," Sierra said, hoping the current reference would help Granna Mae to know they weren't talking about her son.

"I see," she said. "You had an uncle named Paul. Did you know that, Lovey? He had a paper route in Laurel Hurst. One morning he had a flat tire right in the middle of his deliveries, and do you know what he did?"

Everyone was listening to her story, relieved that she was talking about the past in a normal way. Sierra was glad for the diversion, which took the attention off of her.

"Instead of calling home, he pushed that bike the rest of the way, delivering each paper. Then he pushed his bike all the way home in the rain. He was an hour and a half late. I thought he had been kidnapped or worse. Then he walked in that door, and, just imagine, I yelled at him." Granna Mae cut her chicken into an extra small piece and lifted the bite to her lips.

A reverent silence followed.

"You could have called," Mom said, calmed but still determined to make her point. "This is not Pineville. You can't drive around a city this size and think it's completely safe."

"Tawni drives down to Clackamas every day," Sierra said.

"Yes, but we know where she's going, where she'll be, and when she'll be home. If she's late, we know where to start looking. It's completely different from what you did today. You mustn't do that again."

"You can drive back and forth to school, of course," Dad said. "But anywhere else you'll have to clear with us first. Fair enough?"

Since Sierra knew she had the freedom to speak her mind, she charged ahead, letting her feelings out. "Only a week ago I was on the other side of the world, remember? I managed to get myself here from England without any problems. Don't you think I can find my way around Portland?"

"That's not the issue," Dad said. "We all know you're capable of taking care of yourself. Your independence and maturity are beyond your years. Yet, the fact remains, you're sixteen years old. God has entrusted us with your life. Until you're an adult, your mother and I are responsible for giving you boundaries. Whether or not you honor us and our guidelines is, of course, your choice. We try to base our guidelines on what we think is best for you."

"I know," Sierra said with a sigh.

"So, do you agree that you need to check in with your father or myself if you want to drive anywhere other than to school and back?" Mom looked calm now. Sierra wondered if her mom had experienced the same kinds of fears Granna Mae had about Paul. Sierra felt instant remorse that she might have caused that kind of concern.

"Yes, I agree. I realize I should have called. I apologize."

"Good!" Gavin said, pushing away his plate. "Can we have dessert now?"

"In a minute, Gavin," Mom said.

Sierra had only eaten a few bites of her dinner. As she and the rest of the family finished eating, Gavin asked, "What did you do in the library, anyway?"

"I looked around. It's a huge building. I'd like to go there again sometime—with permission, of course."

Mom smiled. "Did you talk with anyone there?"

Sierra started to chuckle. "Only some guy who told me I had a candy wrapper stuck to my rear end."

"And you were walking around like that?" Dad asked.

"Yes!"

Everyone laughed with her.

"Only you, Sierra. Only you," her dad said. "Your mother has visions of you maimed for life in a car accident, but instead you're traipsing about a university library wearing a candy wrapper for a tail. And the guy who told you was probably more embarrassed about it than you were. Am I right?"

"I think so," Sierra said.

Mom went into the kitchen and returned with a plate of cookies and a pitcher of milk. Rather than join the others in eating dessert, Sierra excused herself and went upstairs to her room, promising to return in a few minutes to help with the dishes. She stretched out on her bed and tried to decide what it was that still made her feel unsettled inside.

Things with her parents were smoothed out. Her grandmother seemed to be doing well. She was even getting along with Tawni. Something wasn't right, though.

Was it school? Probably. She flat out didn't want to be in high school anymore. That was it. She wanted to be in college and be around college students like she was in England. That's where she belonged.

Then a vague thought fluttered through her mind. It was something Katie had said one of their last nights at Carnforth. Something about how she was homesick for being in high school. At the time Sierra had thought it was a strange thing to say, but it seemed even stranger now since Sierra couldn't wait to grow up.

Will I be sorry for pushing ahead so fast? Will I wish I took my time and enjoyed high school more?

Sierra still wanted to transfer to the public high school. That way she could slip right in with the crowd. She didn't need to be popular like she was in Pineville. She just wanted this next year and a half to slip by as fast as possible. It would go much faster if she were lost in a school of several thousand students.

Her determination to leave Royal Academy kept her in a monotone sort of mood all the next day. She spoke only when spoken to and then responded as simply as possible. In her mind, all she had to do was finish out the week, as she had agreed to, and then she could discuss with her parents why she should go to public school. They had always been fair about hearing her side of things. Certainly they would agree with her that public school was the best route for her to go.

To make sure there were no wrinkles in her relationship with her parents, Sierra came right home from school on Thursday and even helped her mom give Brutus his bath, all without being asked.

Brutus was a fun-loving Saint Bernard they had owned for the past three years. Even though Sierra wasn't crazy about animals in general, she did love Brutus.

In Pineville, Brutus was the king of the neighborhood. He roamed around freely but always showed up on time for dinner. Everybody in the neighborhood loved Brutus.

Since they had moved to Portland, Brutus had been acting strange. He moped around all day and begged to go inside the boys' clubhouse whenever anyone was in it. Brutus seemed uninterested in checking out the neighborhood or marking his territory.

Mom thought a bath might help. Sierra didn't understand the logic but agreed to assist in the sudsy mess. As soon as they plunged Brutus into the downstairs tub, he turned into a two-hundred-pound jellyfish.

"Come on, boy," Mom coaxed. "You have to help us out here. Stand up so we can scrub you all nice and clean."

The downstairs tub was the original, cast-iron claw foot and was difficult to maneuver around. Brutus filled the entire tub and seemed only interested in licking the faucet with his great pink tongue. Sierra and her mom scrubbed and rubbed and sweet-talked the big guy until the smell of wet dog was almost overpowering in the small bathroom.

"Are we going to dry him off in here?" Sierra asked.

"We could haul him to the kitchen, but I think he would only make more of a mess in there. Let's try it in here." Mom turned off the water after the final rinse.

Getting the big lug over the high sides of the tub was a real challenge. He didn't want to get out. That wasn't like Brutus either. He used to fight his baths in Pineville, and the minute he was freed, he was out of there, shaking like crazy.

"Look at him," Sierra said. "He's turned into a big baby. Come on, Brutus. Lift your paws. That's it. Over the side. Now the back paws. Okay, good. Now you stand right there and let us towel you off."

For the first time in history, Brutus complied.

"It's as if he's depressed," Sierra said, wiping the mellow dog dry.

"Do you think he misses home?" Mom asked.

"How can you make a dog understand that this is his new home?"

"I think he knows," Mom said. "That's why he's bummed. He's mourning the loss. You know what they say about how the bigger they are, the harder they fall. He'll come around. Wes is coming home this weekend, and I'm sure that will perk Brutus up. At least Wes will make sure he exercises."

Sierra's oldest brother was the one who had brought Brutus home three years ago. The dog was only an armful of brown and white fur, with an endearing little pouty face. There was no way anyone could say no to keeping him, especially Sierra's mom, who was a devoted animal lover. Wes had said the dog was for Mom. Since he was going away to college in a month, he wanted Mom to have somebody to fuss over.

"Okay, you big brute," Mom said, grabbing the dog by his collar and leading him out of the house. "It's to the backyard for you. At least you smell better. Maybe you'll start perking up a little too."

Brutus plodded across the cold grass and stopped in front of the workshop's door. No one was inside. He could go through his doggie door if he wanted. But Brutus curled up on the doormat and laid his jowls down on his clean white paws.

Sierra and her mom stood at the kitchen window watching. Sierra thought she could almost hear him sigh.

"Did you know the green ones aren't good to eat?"

Sierra turned around and saw Granna Mae looking at a basket of fruit on the baker's rack by the refrigerator.

"They're okay, Granna Mae," Sierra said, walking over to see what might be in the basket. There were two oranges, three red apples, and one brown spotted banana. "There aren't any green ones in here," she said. "Do you want a red apple?"

"I don't want an apple," Granna Mae said, looking at

Sierra as if she were the one who was confused. She started to hum to herself and walked away.

Sierra and her mom exchanged looks of concern.

"It's so hard to stand by and watch a life thin out like that," Mom said. "I want to stop the clock and turn it back."

Sierra considered commenting on how she wished she could turn the clock forward in her life. She decided to keep that thought to herself. It wouldn't sound right if she said it aloud.

All these thoughts pushed Sierra to do something she had been thinking about for a week. She wrote a letter to Katie. Certainly no one was better than Katie, who would speak her mind and explain to Sierra why she was struggling with this growing up. Sierra also wanted to tell Katie about Paul.

Lying on her stomach across her unmade bed, Sierra wrote on a piece of notebook paper, "Dear Katie, Okay, tell me if you think this is a God-thing or not. When I arrived at Heathrow, I was waiting to use the phone when this guy turned around . . . "

chapter twelve

ON FRIDAY AFTERNOON SIERRA CLEANED out her locker and took all her books home. She thought it would be easier for her mom to withdraw her from the school on Monday if she had all her books to turn in at one time. Sierra felt unemotional about her choice to leave Royal Academy. All week she had distanced herself from everything and everybody, which made it easy to walk away.

Sierra guessed it would help to take home her gym clothes as well. She walked to the girls' dressing room and worked the combination on her locker. Some girls, who were on the other side of the row of tall metal lockers, seemed so involved in their conversation they hadn't noticed that anyone else had come in.

"I think she's stuck-up," one of the girls said.

"That's not a fair judgment, Marissa," the other girl said.

"Well, look at how she has treated us all week. It's like she's too good for us. We're all little peons."

"I think we should give her a chance. Maybe invite

her over with a bunch of girls and see if she opens up."

"She's not going to open up," Marissa said. "I'm telling you, Sierra is totally stuck-up."

It had not begun to register with Sierra that they might be talking about her until Marissa used her name. Then she froze. Who were these girls? What right did they have to form such an incorrect opinion of her? Being a confronter by nature, Sierra stormed around the lockers and stated, "I am *not* stuck-up!"

Both the girls looked stunned. Their mouths dropped, their eyes popped, and neither of them had anything to say. Sierra recognized them from some of her classes. With nothing else to add to her declaration, she turned and marched away, snatching up her gym clothes and storming out the door.

That's it! That is it! I'm out of here. Who do those little prissies think they are, calling me stuck-up? I've never been stuck-up in my life! I'm always the one who makes friends first and fastest. I'm the one who goes out of my way to make each person feel she belongs to the group. I'm not stuck-up. They are! And that's why I'm leaving!

Sierra unlocked the door of the Rabbit and threw her books and gym clothes onto the backseat. She wished this car had more oomph. If it did, she would peel out of that parking lot so fast, those girls in the gym would hear her tires squeal. Unfortunately, the car wasn't made for dramatic displays of emotion. It had difficulty just cranking over when she turned the key. Sierra drove away as fast as she could, telling herself to calm down, shake it off, block the incident from her memory.

By the time she arrived home, she was even more heated up. Stomping into the house, she went right to her room. Tawni was changing clothes for work, which only infuriated Sierra more. She had no place she could go to be alone, no place that was completely hers. She scooped her clothes out of the rocking chair in the corner and heaved them over onto her bed.

"Why are you all bent out of shape?" Tawni asked, cinching a wide black belt around her slim waist.

"I hate it here," Sierra blurted out. "I wish we didn't have to move here. I wish we were back home!"

"Have you even tried to make this place home for yourself?" Tawni asked.

"Of course I have! You can't tell me you like it here better than Pineville." The rocker was empty and ready to soothe her, but Sierra refused to sit down.

"I love it here," Tawni said. "You will too, if you give it a chance. Portland has so much more to offer than Pineville ever did. What set you off?"

"Nothing."

"Oh, and I'm supposed to believe that? Come on. What happened?"

"All right, you want to know? I'll tell you. Those girls at this nice Christian school said I was stuck-up!"

"So have you been?"

"Of course not!"

"Were they friends of yours?"

"I don't have any friends here," Sierra said, surrendering to the rocking chair and folding her arms across her chest.

Tawni flipped her shoulder-length hair back and looked at Sierra. "You know, sometimes you amaze me. You can be so smart and so dumb at the same time, so mature and such a baby. You're really blind to this whole thing, aren't you? If you want to make a friend, you have to be a friend first."

"Duh!" Sierra said, making a face at Tawni. "Maybe I don't want to make any friends here."

"Oh, well that's intelligent!" Tawni grabbed her purse and headed for the door.

"You going to work?" Sierra asked. She couldn't wait to have the room to herself. Yet at the same time, she didn't want her sister to leave. Not yet. Not until she spilled her guts a little more.

"Yes, I'm going to work, and afterwards I'm going out to coffee with two of my *new* friends from the store. Watch and learn, Oh stubborn one. This is how it's done." She opened the door and was about to leave when she turned around to deliver one final jab. "And I've already told Mom and Dad where I'm going and when I expect to be back, even though I don't have to because I'm eighteen."

Sierra picked up a slipper from the floor and heaved it at the door just as Tawni closed it. "And I'm eighteen," Sierra mimicked. She hated being sixteen. Hated, hated, hated it! What a horrible age. Nothing was "sweet sixteen" about it. She could drive, but only to school and back. She had no friends, no social life, nothing to do on a Friday night but feel sorry for herself.

At least back in Pineville she had dozens of friends to hang out with, friends she had earned by working hard to keep the relationships going even when it would have been easier to walk away. Tawni didn't have to give her advice on friendships. Sierra knew all about them and could even teach a seminar on making friends, if anyone ever asked her to. But of course, no one ever asks a sixteen-year-old to do anything.

"Sierra?" Mom called out, gently tapping on her closed door. "Is it all right if I come in?"

"I guess."

Mom opened the door and came in, with Granna Mae right behind her. *Oh great, now I have double counsel. Just what I need!* Sierra didn't mind talking to her mom. And she loved talking things over with Granna Mae sometimes too. But both of them, at the same time, when she was at about the lowest point of her life, felt suffocating.

Granna Mae sat on Tawni's neatly made bed and cast a skeptical glance around at Sierra's mess. Mom pulled out the straight-back chair from the desk and sat facing Sierra about five feet away. They formed a tight little triangle.

"I know, my side of the room is a mess," Sierra said, throwing up a smoke screen to sidetrack both of them. "I'll clean it up this weekend."

"Good," said Mom. "I love it when you clean your room. I did want to talk with you, though, about something else."

Sierra shrugged.

"I've been noticing it's a little tough for you to make the adjustment to moving here. I wanted to know if I could do something to help out."

"You can let me go to the public high school. I don't want to go to Royal. I gave it a week, like you asked. It's not my kind of school."

"And what is your kind of school?" Granna Mae asked.

Sierra felt like saying, "A huge one where I can blend in with the crowd, make it through my next year and a half as soon as possible, and get out of there!" Instead she said, "I'm not sure. But it's not Royal."

"We'll need to talk with Dad about it," Mom said calmly. "I'm sure we'll have some time to do that this weekend. Is there anything else besides school that's bothering you?"

"No."

Mom paused and then said, "Wes should be here in about an hour. I thought we would all go out for pizza tonight. You and Wesley might want to catch a movie afterwards."

As Mom talked, Granna Mae stood up and ambled over to the antique dresser that had been in this room for several decades. She tilted her head and examined her reflection in the beveled mirror above the dresser.

Sierra couldn't help but wonder if she were slipping into one of her time warps.

Granna Mae touched the wrinkled corners of her eyes and looked closer. "Isn't that odd," she said. "Why, just yesterday I was twelve. I'm quite sure of it."

Sierra and Mom exchanged quick looks.

"Or maybe we'll order a couple of pizzas and have them delivered," Mom said quietly. Sierra thought her mother must be concerned about trying to take Granna Mae out to a pizza parlor when she was in a confused state of mind.

"You know," Granna Mae said, turning to face them, "it goes just like that." She snapped her wrinkled fingers and looked at Sierra. "It will come soon enough, Lovey." She headed for the door and said, "I'm going downstairs for a cup of coffee. Do either of you care to join me?"

Now Sierra and her mom were even more surprised. Granna Mae had called her Lovey, an indicator of which time zone she was functioning in. So what was the look in the mirror for and the speech about being twelve only yesterday? Sierra couldn't help but wonder if Granna Mae understood Sierra's passion to be all grown up and was, in her quirky way, trying to tell Sierra to slow down.

"Sure," Mom said, "I'll go with you."

"And I'll clean my room," Sierra said, "which I'm sure will make both of you happy."

"Tawni will be the most delighted," Mom said as she followed Granna Mae out of the room.

Sierra sat in the chair for a while, rocking back and forth. Then she went over to the antique mirror and looked into it closely, the way Granna Mae had. She almost expected it to be an enchanted mirror that would reflect back her image at sixty-eight years old. All she saw was her freckled nose, her wild hair, and blue-gray eyes that were not yet wrinkled. She smiled and tried to wrinkle them up the way her dad's did when he was laughing hard or trying not to cry. She thought it made her look kind of old. She uncrinkled them and looked again.

They are the same color as Paul's, she realized. *That flight attendant was right. We do have the same eyes. If only we saw things from the same perspective.*

Then, as Sierra had done dozens of times that week, she prayed for Paul.

chapter thirteen

"WHAT DO YOU GUYS WANT? PEPPERONI and what else?" Wes stood next to his father at the order window of the Flying Pie Pizzeria and called to the rest of them.

Wes took after Mom's side of the family. He was tall, with lots of wavy brown hair, and a long straight nose. His eyes were like Dad's, brown and crinkly in the corners.

"I want pineapple," Gavin said.

"Olives," said Dillon.

"Why don't we try to find a table?" Mom suggested. "How many are we tonight?"

"Seven," Sierra said, taking a quick count. The room was full, which was probably a sign this was a good place to eat. The women and boys threaded their way to the back of the darkened eating area and managed to find a large booth in the corner. If they could locate an extra chair for the end, they would all fit. This is how it always was when their large family went anywhere. It was frustrating, though, since most places were designed with a family of four in mind.

The pizza parlor was cozy, with red vinyl seats, checkered plastic tablecloths, metal pizza stands on each table, and red patio candles underneath the stands to keep the pizza warm. On the ceiling above Sierra was a table and two chairs hung upside down, complete with tablecloth, plastic food, and even a flower in a vase. It was all securely suspended; yet Sierra wondered if an illusion like that might throw Granna Mae into confusion. She seemed to be doing fine.

Gavin and Dillon came racing to their table, begging for quarters so they could play the video games in the adjoining room.

"I don't have any," Sierra told them after they had hit up Granna Mae and Mom and came up empty. Sierra had on leggings, her cowboy boots, and an oversized gray cowl-neck sweater. She had no pockets, no backpack, and she never carried a purse. She didn't even own one. "Go ask Wes. He'll probably join you in the arcade."

The boys scrambled off to harass their oldest brother, who sometimes acted more like an indulgent uncle to them than a brother. As Sierra predicted, Wes joined the guys and pumped quarters into their machines until their pizzas arrived.

About forty minutes later, after nearly all of the two extra-large pizzas had been devoured, the Jensen troupe left in two cars. Mom, Dad, Granna Mae, and the boys went home while Wes and Sierra headed across town to a movie Wes said he wanted to see.

She didn't say anything all the way to the theater. Wes didn't seem to notice. He had plenty to talk about, such as his truck, his classes at school, and his job stocking grocery shelves on the swing shift. This was his third year at Oregon State University in Corvallis. He was twenty-three, and what Sierra liked most about Wes was that he treated her as an equal.

Wes seemed to know his way around Portland a lot better than Sierra did. She finally opened up and told him how she had gotten lost a few days earlier and ended up at Lewis and Clark.

"So do you think you want to go there next year, or are you going to come down to OSU?" Wes asked.

"I'm only a junior, remember? I have another year and a half before I have to make that decision."

"Oh, yeah, I keep forgetting. Ever since you got your driver's license, I've been thinking of you as about ready to graduate."

"Nope. Not yet. Although it can't be any too soon for me."

"How do you like Portland?"

"It's okay. Tawni likes it here."

They pulled into the parking lot at the movie theater. Sierra hopped out of Wes's truck, and he made sure the doors were locked. Wes's stereo had been stolen from his old car once when it was parked at a friend's apartment complex. Now he was extra careful, especially since he was the one paying for his insurance and truck payments now.

They stood in line to buy tickets, and Sierra shivered in the damp night air. She wished she had a jacket with her. Theaters seemed cold to her. Or maybe it was just that she had the talent of sitting right under the air conditioning vent. As they walked in, Sierra involuntarily shivered again. Her brother put his arm around her and rubbed her arm to warm her up. They had to wait a minute while a herd of moviegoers exited the show that had just concluded in the theater next to theirs.

As they stood waiting, Wes squeezed her a little closer and said in her ear, "It's sure good to see you, Sierra. I'm glad you had a good time in England and that you got home safely."

Sierra smiled up at her brother with sincere admiration. "Thanks," she said.

Then the image of a brown felt hat caught in the corner of her eye. Sierra snapped her head away from Wes and scanned the trail of people moving past them. There, only ten feet away, was Paul. He kept on walking with the stream of people, but his head was turned, and he was staring at Sierra. She stared right back.

"Did you see somebody you know?" Wes asked, removing his arm from around her shoulder.

"Yeah."

"Do you want to go say hi? We have a few minutes before the movie starts."

Sierra didn't know what to do. Should she run after him? He was already out the door. What if someone were with him—like Jalene? Sierra hadn't noticed anyone.

If he wanted to talk to me, she reasoned, *he certainly could have stopped and said hi.*

Then she remembered that Wes had had his arm around her and was talking softly in her ear while Paul walked by. It must have looked as if Wes were her boyfriend.

"Do you want me to go with you, wait here, get us some seats, or what?" Wes asked.

"Let's go in," Sierra said. "I don't think I could catch him."

They started down the carpeted hallway. "Do you want some popcorn?" Sierra asked.

"Are you kidding? After all that pizza? How could you possibly have room for anything else?"

"Actually, my stomach feels kind of empty right now. Can I have some money?"

Wes, playing his role of benevolent uncle, pulled a five-dollar bill from his pocket and said, "Get a large drink, too, and I'll split it with you. Just not orange. I'll save you a seat."

Sierra stood in line at the snack bar but kept looking out the windows that lined the front of the theater, wondering if by any remote chance Paul were still out there. Maybe if he saw her alone he would come back inside and say something to her. She knew it was a crazy thing to think.

The more she thought about it, it was crazy that she had even seen him. What are the chances of the two of them connecting in this huge city? To have seen Jalene at the gas station and now Paul at the movies was unsettling.

Katie might call it a God-thing, and it was insofar as it made Sierra think about Paul and then, consequentially, pray for him. However, Sierra thought the chance encounters were more like a "weird thing" or a "crazy-making thing." Why should she be so connected with this guy?

"May I help you?" the girl behind the counter asked.

"A medium buttered popcorn and a large Coke."

"We don't have Coke. Is Pepsi okay?"

"Sure. Fine." Sierra felt as if people shouldn't be allowed to ask such stupid questions, especially when she was so deep in her thoughts about Paul and all the bizarre encounters they had had. Coke, Pepsi, what difference did it make?

"That will be $6.50," the girl said.

"Six dollars and fifty cents? For a Coke and a popcorn?"

"Pepsi and popcorn," the girl corrected her.

"Forget it. I'll just have the Co . . . Pepsi. I don't want the popcorn." Sierra held out the five-dollar bill. In exchange she received a huge drink, loaded with ice, and two crumpled one-dollar bills. "It's a racket!" Sierra spouted as she turned to go. "I mean, I know you just work here and everything and it's not your fault, but the snack prices are ridiculous."

She marched off, shaking her head. She didn't care that the people in line behind her had heard everything.

All she wanted to do was find Wes, sit down, and get caught up in the movie. She needed to relax.

Then it occurred to her that she wasn't on edge because of the popcorn prices. She had paid that much before and never flinched. Seeing Paul was what had rattled her. She had transferred all those emotions to the price of popcorn.

"Where's the popcorn?" Wes asked when she slid across from him to take her seat. He always wanted to sit on the end of the row.

"I changed my mind. Here's your change. And I got Pepsi. Is that okay?"

"They didn't have Coke, I take it."

"What does it matter?" Sierra barked.

"Whoa!" Wes said, leaning back and taking a hard look at her. "What's up with you?"

"Nothing. Sorry." Sierra settled back in her seat. The movie began, and she was ready to relax.

Only one problem. The movie was centered around spies and skydiving and a high-speed motorcycle race. It was so suspenseful that Sierra was on the edge of her seat the entire two hours. She walked out of the theater with cramped toes from having curled them up inside her boots for most of the movie.

"Great show, don't you think?" Wes asked as they left.

"Sure was full of action. I didn't know I could hold my breath for so long."

"How long?" Wes asked, opening the truck door for her.

"Oh, about two hours."

Wes laughed. "Weren't the special effects amazing when the guy landed in the water, got himself out of the handcuffs, and then released the parachute?"

Sierra nodded. "It was a good movie. Thanks for taking me, Wes."

"Do you want to go anywhere for coffee?"

"No, I'm ready to go home. Are you?"

"Sure. I brought a ton of reading home with me. It would be good if I could chip away at some of it tonight."

Sierra went right to bed when they reached home. Her room was nice and clean after the hour she had spent on it that afternoon.

Putting away her clothes had been more of an anchor than she had realized it would be. As long as her things were scattered around and her luggage from England hadn't been unpacked yet, she had felt her time in this room was only temporary. But once she had put things away and hung her clothes alongside all her other clothes, which the moving fairies had brought to this closet while she was sleeping on the other side of the world, then her stay in this room became permanent. She wasn't sure if that was good or bad.

Tawni would be glad the room was clean, and that was a good thing. She wasn't home yet after going out with her friends from work.

Of course she likes it here. She got to move her belongings into our room and put everything right where she wanted it. She's been here a month, and I've only been here a week. I feel as if everyone is settled, but here I am, walking into the middle of this new life and running to catch up.

Sierra read her Bible until her eyelids became too heavy to stay open. She turned off the light and lay in bed flossing her teeth with an extra-long strand of peppermint-flavored dental floss she had found while unpacking her things.

In the dark, in the silence, the confusing thoughts came tumbling down around her all at once. Like a mental kaleidoscope, the thoughts twirled from hearing the girls in the locker room call her stuck-up, to the image of Granna Mae looking for her youth in the bedroom mirror, to that locked-in stare of Paul's. First in London at the money exchange booth, then on the plane, then at baggage claim, then again tonight, he had stared at her. Why?

Sierra wondered if somehow her matching eyes were like a mirror to him. He was searching for something. What was it?

All she could do was pray for him. And she did. Like a determined warrior with sword drawn, Sierra prayed that God would protect Paul. She prayed that the enemy would release his hold on Paul's life. She prayed that Paul would break up with Jalene or that Jalene would become a Christian. And Sierra prayed that Paul would be miserable until he got back into a really tight relationship with God. Sierra prayed and prayed until she finally felt her shoulders start to relax. Time to retreat. Enough battle for one day.

Tawni entered their room, and Sierra pretended to be asleep.

chapter fourteen

S IERRA HAD ALWAYS LIKED HER PARENTS'
openness and the way she could discuss things
with them, even difficult or embarrassing
things. So she was caught off guard when she talked
with them about leaving Royal Academy, and they
asked her to try it for one more week.

"But, Mom, you said I should try it for one week.
I did, and I don't like it."

"We aren't convinced you gave it a fair try. It was
your first week in Portland, right after your big trip.
You didn't have any time to even settle into your
room." Dad spoke in a direct yet gentle voice. "We need
you to be fair, Sierra. Fair to yourself, fair to the other
students, and fair to us. If we were sure you had actually done that, we would send you over to Madison in
a minute. One more week. And be fair all the way
around this time, okay?"

Wes walked into the kitchen just then, zipping up his
jacket. "I'm going to take Brutus for a walk. Anyone
want to go with me?"

"I do," Sierra said, hopping off the "hot seat" counter stool and hurrying to duck out of this conversation. She was close to saying something she might regret later, and since she had done that so many times, she was beginning to learn it was better to walk away and think things over.

"Get your jacket. It's cold this afternoon. Did anyone hear the weather? Are we expecting snow?"

"I haven't heard," Dad said.

Sierra left the room and returned with a jacket and gloves a few minutes later.

"I hope you can coax Brutus out of his slump," Mom said. "He just hasn't been himself since we moved here."

"Looks to me like he's not the only one," Wes said.

"And what's that supposed to mean?" Sierra said, not sure if he meant her or not.

"Moving is high stress," Wes replied, looking over his shoulder at her. "It's right up there with a death in the family or a job loss on the scale of how much a person's emotions can handle. We saw this chart in my human development class. It's really interesting to see the things that cause stress. Even term papers are on the list. And since that's my biggest source of stress right now, I thought I'd try to downshift a little and relieve some of the stress by walking the dog. You ready, Sierra?"

"I'm ready. I have my own areas of stress to walk off. Let's go."

"Think about what we've been discussing," Dad said as they left. "We'll talk about it some more this weekend, Sierra."

"Okay. And will you guys think about my side of it too?"

"Of course," Dad said. "By the way, I want my shirt back."

"You never wear this old flannel shirt," Sierra said. The ends of the red plaid shirt stuck out from underneath her jeans jacket, and she tugged on them to make her point. "I found it in a mound of clothes in the basement. I thought you were giving it away."

"It was in the mending pile. It's missing a button." Dad shot a teasing glance at Mom, who shrugged her shoulders.

Sierra hadn't noticed the missing button since she had on a thermal undershirt and wore the shirt like a jacket over it. But she knew what Dad's look meant. Mom had many fine abilities, but mending was not one of them. As long as Sierra could remember, Dad had been the one to go to with a missing button or a broken zipper. Mom tried, of course, to do her share of the clothes repair, but sometimes it took months before she got around to the pile of maimed clothing.

"Then may I have your blue work shirt?" Sierra asked.

Dad looked at Mom and said, "I never dreamed I'd be fighting with one of my daughters over *my* clothes."

"Why don't you try some of those thrift stores down on Hawthorne?" Mom asked Sierra.

Sierra remembered that one girl the first day of school saying she bought her jumper at some vintage store on Hawthorne. What was the name of it? "Maybe

I will after we take Brutus out. Do you want to go with me, Mom?"

"Ask me when you're about ready to go, okay?"

Sierra joined Wes in the backyard where he was roughing up Brutus's fur and growling back at his old pal. "Come on, Brute Boy. Let's take Sierra for a walk." He hooked the leash onto Brutus's collar, and the big dog "ruffed" his agreement. They took off down the street with Brutus stopping every two seconds to sniff and scope out the neighborhood.

"I can see this is going to take all afternoon," Sierra said. It was so cold she could see her breath. Her jeans jacket was too thin, and she could feel the damp chill right through the flannel shirt and thermals.

"This is good for him. I think he's been such a slug because he didn't know the neighborhood. I'm taking him on a round of social calls."

Brutus did seem to enjoy the romp. He growled through the fence at the bulldog three houses down, and the two exchanged their greetings in doggie language. Sierra could hear another dog across the street yipping.

"Looks as if a little one over there is trying to get in the act," she said. Wes tugged on the leash, and Brutus gladly galloped across the street to sniff and bark at the little black and white fur ball behind the chain-link fence.

For almost an hour, Wes and Sierra trailed after Brutus as he terrorized the neighborhood dogs. He seemed to be rebounding back to his old self.

Sierra was shivering, and her teeth were chattering as they rounded the corner that led to Granna Mae's grand white house. It was one of the largest houses on the block and certainly the one with the most personality. Two elms stood like silent guards between the front porch and the street. For more than eighty years they had stood their post, shading the elegant white lady in the summer and showering her with amber jewels in the autumn.

Sierra had to admit that she did love this old house. As a child it had seemed like a castle. She and her brothers and sister used to call it "Granna Mae's mansion."

When they came for their visit each summer, Sierra pretended this was really her house, and she would play that she lived there in the horse and buggy days. Iron rings were still fixed in the cement at the curb where nearly a century ago the residents would tie up their horses. Sierra and Tawni once tied their bikes to the rings with their jump ropes. Granna Mae played right along, coming out to the curb with several lumps of sugar in her apron pocket, which she pretended to feed to the horses.

Now Sierra was experiencing her childhood dream of living in this wonderful mansion, and yet she didn't want to be here.

"Come on, Brutus. You've had enough for one day. And if you haven't, I certainly have!" Wes said, leading the dog into the backyard and taking off the leash. Brutus acted as if he weren't through exploring the neighborhood. He bounded over to the gate and barked a few times. Then he thundered to the other side of the yard and barked at some squirrels, who were chittering at the top of the neighbor's tree.

"What did you do to him?" Mom asked, opening the back door and welcoming them into the warm house. It smelled like cinnamon, and Sierra was instantly hungry.

"What are you making?"

"Apple cobbler. How did you manage to revive Brutus?"

"We just took him around to meet his new neighbors," Wes said, opening the oven to peek inside at the cobbler. What Mom lacked in sewing abilities, she made up for in baking. Apple cobbler was Wes's favorite. "You're the world's best mother! When will it be ready?"

"In about fifteen minutes. Why don't you two have some lunch first? Some turkey is in the fridge for sandwiches."

"I think I'll make some soup," Sierra said. Her throat was feeling raw, and she was still cold from the walk.

"After your soup do you want to explore a couple of thrift stores?" Mom asked. "Granna Mae just went upstairs for a nap so I think this would be a good time."

"Sure!" Sierra was always up for exploring, especially a secondhand clothing store. "Let's just go now. I can eat something when we come back."

"Okay. Wes, I know I can count on you to take the cobbler out on time, right? I'll grab my purse. Do you have any money?"

"I have fifteen. I'll get it." Sierra took the stairs two at a time and breathlessly opened her bedroom door.

"Where are you going?" Tawni asked. She was sitting at the desk, doing her fingernails.

"To some thrift stores. Mom is going with me. Do you want to come?" Sierra knew it was pointless to ask Tawni such a question. She only wore clothes from the finest department stores. Her idea of a bargain was a sale in the Spiegel catalog.

Tawni answered politely for once. "No, thanks. Have fun!"

Sierra grabbed her cash and dashed down the stairs. Mom was waiting for her, wearing a full-length coat, gloves, and her favorite paisley scarf. Sierra considered changing into a warmer jacket but didn't. She reasoned it would be warmer in the car once the heater got going.

It wasn't. They drove the van, and its heater took forever to produce any warmth. It was barely puffing out a few breaths of heat when they arrived at the first thrift store. Now Sierra was really chilled.

The shop was full of great items, but it was cold inside the building. Sierra felt her enthusiasm for shopping begin to drain away. But, stubborn as she was, she didn't bend away from her goal. She stuck it out through three stores and spent her entire fifteen dollars plus another eight of Mom's.

The best stuff they found was in the last shop, called A Wrinkle in Time. She remembered this was the store that girl had mentioned the first day of school. And that girl, whatever her name was, had been right. The store had a fantastic collection of low-priced, unique clothes that were Sierra's style. She wished she had a bundle of money so she could buy everything she liked.

In the end, Sierra came home with a black velvet hat, a cream-colored crocheted vest, two men's flannel shirts, and a long skirt from Bangladesh that had two tiny bells on the drawstring at the waist. She thought she would show the girl at school the hat she had found, but then she remembered she wasn't going back to Royal on Monday, if she got her way. Sierra carried her treasures up to her room and laid them out on her bed.

"Let's see what you bought," Tawni said from her curled-up position on the padded window seat. She was reading a fat paperback novel and had on her silly glasses that made Sierra want to laugh. Tawni was the sort of person who would die if anyone important to her ever knew she wore glasses to read.

Sierra popped the hat on first and tilted it to the side.

"That's actually cute," Tawni said. "And those are in style now. You bought it at a thrift store?"

"It was a recycled clothing place. It could be new. I don't know."

"Don't you want to spray it with Lysol or something before you put it on your head?" Tawni looked slightly disgusted.

Sierra ignored her and held up the rest of her finds.

When she showed off the skirt, she said, "This is one of those you wash by hand and then dry by wringing it out to keep the crinkles in it. No ironing necessary. My kind of skirt, don't you think?"

"It smells funny," Tawni said. "Make sure you wash all that stuff before you wear it. It could be full of fleas or lice or worse."

"Don't worry," Sierra said. "I'll wash it all right now. I always do, don't I?"

"I guess. By the way, I wanted to say thanks for cleaning up the room yesterday. I appreciate it."

"I thought you might." Sierra took off the hat, pulled her hair back, and fastened it in a ponytail with a big clip. "You must hate having to live with me," Sierra said. "No two people in the world are more opposite than you and me."

Tawni shrugged and went back to reading her book.

"May I ask you something?"

"Hmm?" Tawni didn't look up.

"What are you going to do when you find your birth mother?"

Tawni looked up slowly and peered at Sierra from over the top of her glasses. It seemed as if she were trying to decide how much of an answer she could trust her little sister with. "I don't know. Talk to her. Find out a few things, such as my medical history, who my father is, and why she gave me up for adoption."

"You're not going to move in with her or anything, are you?"

"Of course not! What a ridiculous question. She obviously didn't want me eighteen years ago. Why would she want me now?"

"Maybe she *did* want you but couldn't keep you," Sierra suggested. "I think if I were you, I'd do the same thing. I'd try to find my biological mother. I just don't know what I'd do with the relationship after I reestablished it."

"I don't either."

"What do you think she's like?"

"I have no idea. Hopefully I'll find out soon. I've got to save up some money first. My new car wiped me out financially. You're lucky you don't have to worry about all that stuff, Sierra. You just wait. These next two years are the cruise years."

"I know," Sierra said. "But I'll bet being older isn't as bad as you make it sound."

"Just wait until you see what kind of responsibility comes with being an adult. Right now you have it easy. You don't have to pay for your own car or car insurance, you don't have to worry about getting a job, and you don't have to start thinking about whether or not to rent your own apartment. Enjoy it while you can, little girl. It goes way too fast."

chapter fifteen

*E*ARLY SUNDAY EVENING SIERRA BROUGHT up the topic of school again with her dad. He was paying bills at the big rolltop desk in the library and had on his favorite CD of classical Bach. She hadn't planned on talking to him yet, but Tawni had brought up the remote phone into their bedroom and asked Sierra if she would mind letting her have some privacy for about an hour.

Sierra had been sitting on the bedroom floor, shuffling through a box of her possessions that hadn't been unpacked yet. She was making two piles, one of things to keep and one of things to throw away.

She left her mess and ambled down the hall to Granna Mae's room. The only TV in the house was in her grandma's room since the family was waiting for Dad to finish the entertainment center before they bought a new one for the downstairs den. Dillon and Gavin were sitting on Granna Mae's bed watching a cartoon special, and Granna Mae was dozing off, stretched out on the love seat in the rounded window alcove.

This was the most charming room in the house. A fire danced in the hearth to the right of the alcove.

Grabbing a quilt from the end of the bed, Sierra slipped over to the love seat and covered up Granna Mae. As she gently tucked the blanket around her grandmother, a little smile crept up Granna Mae's face.

"The Lord thy God," Granna Mae muttered without opening her eyes, "in the midst of thee is mighty. He will rest in His love."

Sierra planted a tiny kiss on Granna Mae's forehead and finished off the verse, whispering, "He will joy over thee with singing."

Then, heading for the door, she told her brothers, "You guys wake up Granna Mae when your show is over so she can get in her own bed."

"She said she didn't mind if we sat on it," Gavin said.

"I know. She doesn't mind a bit. I'm sure she's glad for the company. It's just not good for her to sleep all night on the couch curled up like that."

"We'll wake her," Dillon promised.

Sierra left them and wandered downstairs. That's how she ended up in the library with her dad. She plopped down in the overstuffed chair by the French doors that led to the back deck. This chair was fast becoming her favorite spot in the house. Usually no one was in the library. It smelled old and musty from all the books that were stacked on the floor-to-ceiling shelves. To the left of the chair was a broad-hearthed fireplace with a thick mantel. On the mantel was an antique clock that ticktocked steadily in the silent room. It sounded every hour with a dainty chime that reminded Sierra of an ice cream truck.

"How are you doing, honey?" Dad asked without looking up from his paperwork.

"Okay. I wanted to talk to you some more when you want to take a break. You don't have to stop what you're doing."

Dad put down his pen, turned down the CD player, and turned to face her. Leaning back in the swivel captain's chair, Dad said, "This is a good time. The bills can wait. What do you want to talk about?"

"School."

He tilted his head to the side and folded his arms across his chest. If Sierra were reading his body language correctly, he was indicating to her that he was a rock in his decision.

"I feel strongly about not going back to Royal. If I go one more week, it will only prolong the inevitable and make it harder for me to make the switch."

"And what will make the switch harder?" Dad asked.

The truth was she didn't feel nearly as convinced of her decision as she had on Friday. She had found herself thinking about some of the students this weekend, and she wondered about their lives. Like Randy. What was his dad doing in Nepal when he bought that coat? And those girls in the locker room. Surely they must think she was a jerk for the way she acted on Friday.

She was beginning to wish she could apologize to
them. Sierra hated unresolved relationships.

Another reason she felt mellowed about going to
Royal was Brutus. She found that she and Brutus had
a lot in common. In Pineville, Brutus was the most
popular dog in the neighborhood. In Portland, he was
nobody. Then Wes took him around the neighborhood
and helped him break the ice, so to speak, with all the
dogs on the block. Sierra had thought during their
walk that she had withdrawn and felt sorry for herself,
just as Brutus had. She had convinced herself the solution was to withdraw more and hide in a huge school.
Now she wondered if maybe she needed to "make the
rounds" and get acquainted at Royal. It would be a lot
harder now, since she had proved to those two girls
that she was stuck-up by yelling at them that she wasn't
stuck-up.

"I don't know," she finally said to her dad. "I'm mixed
up about the whole thing. I don't know what I want."

Dad unfolded his arms and leaned forward. "Do you
know what, honey? None of us really gave a thought to
how hard this transition would be for you. You went
from a life-changing experience in Europe to an instant
new home and new school all within a few days. You've
held up remarkably well."

"I don't know about that," Sierra said.

"Wes got me thinking about it when he mentioned
that stress list yesterday. You've had double, no, triple
the changes. The rest of us had a three-week head start

on you. Somehow we expected you to fall right in line with where we were in this transition. I can understand why it seems confusing. And that's why I believe we should stick with our original choice, which you made with us almost two months ago. I think you should give Royal another try."

Sierra let out a sigh. She knew her dad was right. But she found it hard to concede. "Okay," she said at last.

Then it hit Sierra that she had homework. When she was sure she wasn't going back, she had mentally written off the assignment.

"Thanks for talking to me about it," Sierra said.

"Any time," Dad replied, twirling the chair back to the desk.

"Good night." She hurried back upstairs. Tawni was still on the phone and made a face when Sierra entered.

Sierra snatched her backpack and headed for the kitchen, hoping she could remember which chapters she was supposed to read. She was fortunate to snag the last piece of Mom's apple cobbler. Then, pouring herself a glass of milk and warming the cobbler in the microwave, Sierra planted herself on a kitchen stool and spread her books out across the counter. That's when she remembered she needed book covers for all of them as well.

It was a lot easier when I thought I wasn't going back. I can't believe I changed my mind so easily. Maybe Dad is right. Maybe I've been under more stress than I realized, and that's what made me act stuck-up to those girls.

Sierra decided the first thing she would do tomorrow at school would be to find those girls and apologize. But, when Sierra woke up the next morning, her throat was so swollen she could barely swallow.

"I'm not faking it," she told her mom after dragging herself downstairs and turning on the tea kettle. "My head is pounding, my ears are stopped up, and it hurts to swallow."

"You're past the age where I decided whether or not you can make it to school. You decide for yourself."

"I can't go. I feel awful."

"Probably jet lag," Dillon said, as if he knew all about it.

"It's not jet lag, Dillon. You don't get jet lag a week and a half after you've been somewhere. I'm coming down with the flu or a cold or something." The tea kettle began to whistle, and Sierra poured herself a cup of lemon herbal tea and dipped in a spoonful of honey. Then, carrying it upstairs with shaky hands, she went back to bed.

Tawni was already gone. She had a seven o'clock class on Mondays at the junior college.

With the room to herself, Sierra closed the door and headed for her snug bed. On the floor sat her unfinished project from the evening before—packing box, paper, and two piles of her things. Tawni would be ticked off, but she would have to walk around it for another day. All Sierra could do was crawl back into bed.

Something happens to a person's imagination when she's sick. For Sierra, the morning turned into a strange limbo between fast-paced, no time to think it through reality and wild, worst-case-scenario dreams. One of her bizarre episodes included Paul. Jalene was standing next to him at the library, kissing him the way she had at the airport. Paul turned into a robot and followed her up and down the aisles, carrying her books. Jalene kept piling on the books until Paul couldn't carry any more.

Then, in her dazed imagination, Sierra arrived on the scene, driving a super mobile shaped like a huge Mars bar. She was steering it up and down the library rows, chasing Jalene.

When Sierra forced her eyes open and scanned the bedroom for familiar things, she could feel the perspiration forming on her forehead. All she wanted was a nice hot bath. That triggered another round of crazy imaginings in which she was trying to bathe Brutus. But he ended up putting her in the tub, and with his great, furry paw, he was lathering her hair. Then Brutus was walking her to school and coaxing her to make friends with students who were behind chain-link fences, yipping at her.

A cool hand on her forehead drew her back to reality. She opened her eyes.

"How are you feeling, Lovey? I brought you something for your throat." Granna Mae nudged Sierra to sit up and receive the glass of dark green liquid held out to her. One of her grandmother's herbal concoctions, no doubt. Sierra knew it was harmless. Still, it could be nasty-tasting, and she wished she could somehow turn it down without hurting her grandmother's feelings.

Knowing it would be rude to plug her nose, Sierra did her best to hold her breath and chug the liquid down her swollen throat. The aftertaste made her shiver. "Is there any water in here?" She knew her tea was gone but wondered if she had brought up a glass of water and had forgotten it.

"I'll get you one, Lovey." Off Granna Mae padded to fetch a drink of water.

Sierra waited and waited. The remedy began to taste fermented. Finally she couldn't stand it any longer and forced herself to venture down the hall to the bathroom and get her own drink. Walking only made her head spin more. She barely made it back to her bed before her headache overpowered her.

A few minutes later her mom walked in with a glass of orange juice and a thermometer.

"Thanks," Sierra said, eagerly sipping the orange juice. "Did Granna Mae tell you I asked for a cup of water?"

"No. Was she up here?"

"About ten minutes ago."

"That's odd. She's been rather mixed up this morning. Did she know it was you?" Mom asked.

Sierra thought hard. "I'm pretty sure she called me Lovey. She gave me a glass of some green stuff to drink."

"You didn't drink it, did you?" Mom looked stunned.

"Yes." Suddenly Sierra realized she couldn't assume anything with her grandmother anymore. For all she knew, Granna Mae had fed her plant food or the soaking solution for her dentures. "Wasn't too smart, was it? I thought it was one of her vitamin or herbal drinks."

"It very well may have been, but we can't be sure about anything with her. Did you say she gave it to you ten minutes ago?"

"About that."

"Well, if it were poison you would know it by now."

"Great," Sierra said, placing the orange juice on her night stand. Then, because she wasn't too sick to play a joke on her mom, Sierra suddenly bulged out her eyes and clutched her throat. With a gasp and a wheeze, she closed her eyes and flopped lifeless onto her pillow.

"Very funny," Mom said. "I take it you're feeling better."

"Actually, I kind of am."

"Must be the orange juice."

"Or Granna Mae's green gunk. Can we at least try to find out what it was? I can't believe I drank it. I didn't want to hurt her feelings."

"Here," Mom said, leaving the thermometer. "I'll check on Granna Mae. Take your temperature and let me know what it is."

It was only 99 degrees, a slight fever but not one that warranted a trip to the doctor. Sierra fell back asleep. This time it was a deep, restorative, dreamless sleep.

Tuesday she had a hard time deciding if she should

attend school or not. Mom had left the choice up to her. Sierra missed the days of grade school when her mom would stick the thermometer in Sierra's mouth and then look at her watch, waiting for it to reveal its secret. She would pull it out and read the secret message inside the glass tube that only moms could read. If it was bent to Sierra's favor, Mom would say, "Stay in bed today." If not, Mom would say, "I think you can make it." That thermometer was as much of a mystery to Sierra in her childhood as the groundhog seeing his shadow. In her mind, the thermometer made the decision about school or no school. Not Sierra. Not her mom.

Now it was all up to Sierra. She was beginning to feel the reality of Tawni's comments about having more responsibilities the older she became. She decided to go to school.

Sierra settled on jeans and a flannel shirt with her thick hunter's jacket and new velvet hat. She drove herself to school so she could leave if she felt too sick.

As soon as she had made a trip to her locker, Sierra waited in the hallway until she spotted the girls from the gym last Friday. She saw one of them and made eye contact. The girl immediately looked away and kept walking to her locker.

Sierra marched up to her and said, "Excuse me." The girl looked timid. "I just want to apologize for the way I acted Friday. I was a jerk, and you were right. I did act stuck-up last week. I'm really sorry. I hope we can start over."

The girl looked surprised but relieved. She had silky brown hair parted down the middle and tucked behind each ear. She wore tiny pearl earrings and had thin eyebrows above green eyes. "Sure," she said. "My name's Vicki. Don't worry about Friday. Marissa and I were out of line to talk about you behind your back. I'm sorry."

"That's okay," Sierra said. "It was actually a God-thing because it made me realize what I was doing."

"'A God-thing,'" Vicki repeated with a smile. "That's good. Did you make that up?"

"No. A friend I met in England."

"You've been to England?" Vicki asked. Before Sierra could answer, Vicki was motioning to someone over Sierra's shoulder. Marissa joined them, chewing on her lower lip as if she were in trouble.

"I want to apologize," Sierra said again. "I was out of line Friday, and I'm sorry I acted the way I did."

"It's okay," Marissa said. "We were wrong for gossiping about you. I'm sorry, too."

"I was hoping we could all start over."

"Good idea," said Marissa. She smiled but didn't show her teeth. Marissa was shorter than Sierra. She had on a denim jacket and wore her medium-length, cinnamon-colored hair in a loose ponytail.

"Sierra was saying she's been to England," Vicki said.

Just then another girl walked up to them and said loudly, "I don't believe it! This time you have to say you bought it at A Wrinkle in Time."

Sierra turned to see the girl who had worn the matching patchwork dress Sierra's first day. Today she had on
the same black velvet hat as Sierra's. Sierra laughed. "I
did," she said. "On Saturday. When did you buy yours?"

"Last Thursday," the girl said. "By the way, if you
want the notes from English yesterday, I have them
with me. I noticed you weren't there."

"Thanks. I'm sorry; I don't remember your name."

"Amy," the girl answered. She looked Italian, with
thick black hair and dark, expressive eyes. The hat
looked really cute on her. Sierra wondered if it looked
that good on her.

"Amy, I want to apologize to you too, about acting so
stuck-up last week. I'm trying to make a fresh start."

"Then you're at the right school because the people
here are very good at forgiving." She shot a sideways
glance at Marissa and, still smiling, said, "Most of the
time."

chapter sixteen

"**Y**OU WERE RIGHT," SIERRA SAID WHEN she arrived home that afternoon. "I was wrong. I stand corrected. There, do you feel better?"

Mom was standing at the kitchen sink, scrubbing potatoes. "Let's see, could it be you enjoyed school?"

Sierra poured herself some cranberry juice and sat on a stool by the kitchen counter. "I apologized to everyone I thought I'd been a brat to, and they treated me as if I were a totally different person."

"Probably because you treated them like different people," Mom suggested.

"My throat even feels better," Sierra said.

"Sounds like a wonderful day for you all around."

"How was your day?"

"Good. Granna Mae had a doctor's appointment. I talked with him some after she left the room. He seems to think a lot of the disorientation last week was due to the move and changing things around in her house and in her bedroom. She might be doing a little better now that we're all together in one place without any more major changes for a while."

"That's encouraging."

"Oh, and a letter came for you today." Mom motioned with her head. "It's on the front entry table."

"Thanks. Do you want some help with dinner?"

"No, I'm fine, thanks. I might take you up on the offer after dinner."

Sierra placed her emptied glass on the counter and went in search of her letter. She guessed it might be from one of her friends in Pineville. She was pleasantly surprised to see it was from Katie. Carrying the thick envelope into the library, Sierra curled up in her favorite chair and began to read.

"Hey, Sierra! How are you doing as you readjust to real life? My first week was hard. I don't think I was much fun to be around. I've mellowed out now that I'm back in the routine of school at Palomar Junior College.

"I went down to San Diego this weekend to see Doug and go to the God Lovers' Bible Study that meets at his apartment. Boy, the stories I could tell you about that place! I'll save those for another time, like this summer when we get together.

"Anyway, Doug gave me this letter to send on to you. A guy named Jeremy at the Bible study gave it to him and asked him to get it to you."

Sierra pulled the folded-up envelope out of Katie's envelope and looked at the handwriting. All that was written across the front was "Sierra" in bold black letters.

She wanted to rip it open, but read the rest of Katie's letter for a clue.

"I'm dying of curiosity, Sierra. You'll have to write me immediately and tell me who wrote this mystery letter to you. I can't help but think it's from that Paul guy you wrote and told me about.

"Well, stop wasting your time reading this nothing letter from me and read the mystery letter! Then write me and tell me all about it.

"Oh, and one more thing. You asked about what I meant about being homesick for being a teen again. I'd give anything to be sixteen again. I was a dork so much of the time because I kept trying to be more independent. My parents kept putting a halt to that. They wouldn't even let me be a counselor at summer camp for one measly week! I used to think their decisions to hold me back from doing all these wild, independent things were because they aren't Christians and most of the things I wanted to do were with my Christian friends or with the church youth group. Now I think I understand that they just wanted me to take it slow and stay home as much as possible. I'm the youngest of three kids, and so I guess they wanted me to stay anchored a little longer.

"I don't know if that answers your question, but if you want some free advice, take each day as slowly as you can and enjoy it when you can find simple solutions to your day-to-day problems. Believe me, it only gets more complicated from here on out!

"Hey, are you still reading this? Why? Open that letter! I hold you in my heart, Katie (Phil. 1:7)."

Sierra carefully tore open the sealed back of the envelope. She had to admire Katie. If she had been the designated courier for a mystery letter, she couldn't guarantee her curiosity wouldn't keep her from trying to see who the letter was from.

Sierra pulled out one sheet of nice-quality paper. The writing was in bold, black ink and was a mixture of printing and cursive. It was signed "Paul."

Feeling as if her heart were pounding fiercely in her already tight throat, Sierra swiftly read the letter. Then she read it again, letting each word sink in.

"Sierra, You've ruined my entire life. Are you happy now? I couldn't sleep for two days after I got back. Jet lag, I'm sure. Or was it the angels of torture you sent to harass me? Well, they did their job. I broke up with Jalene and walked away with my honor. Then I even went to church last Sunday for the first time in ten months. I imagine you're smiling right now. Feeling quite proud of yourself, are you? Well, don't give yourself any medals yet. I'm still on the fence. Only now my back is probably turned in the right direction. My mother thinks you're an angel. I told her you're only a little girl with a smart mouth. You don't fly, do you? Paul."

At the very bottom, in small letters, was a post office box number. Sierra interpreted that as an invitation to respond, especially since he ended his letter with a question.

Sierra folded the letter in her lap and tried to slow down her rapid breathing.

He must have written this last week if he sent it to his brother in San Diego, and I received it before Sunday. So why didn't he say anything about seeing me at the movies?

Then Sierra remembered that when Paul saw her, Wes had his arm around her. Paul obviously thought Wes was her boyfriend. She liked the idea of Paul thinking she was going out with a guy who was obviously older than she. Seven years, to be exact. She sat for a long time, lost in her thoughts.

When Mom called her to come for dinner, Sierra folded the letter, which she had now read at least fifteen times, and ran it up to her room. Tawni wasn't there. Sierra tucked it under her pillow, and as she did, she remembered how one of the girls in England talked about writing letters to her future husband and keeping them in a shoe box under her bed. Maybe Sierra would do that too one of these days.

On her way to the door, she tripped over her piles of stuff on the floor and told herself she had to pick it up right after dinner.

All through the meal, Sierra's imagination was floating somewhere above the table, weaving in and out of the antique chandelier from Denmark. She decided she would write Paul tonight, before she had time to change her mind. She would be witty and brief. Just enough of a note to let him know she could return the volley with ease.

There was a slight problem, though, she suddenly realized. She didn't know his last name. He didn't write it, and Katie didn't mention what Jeremy's last name was. Would the letter be delivered to a post office box without a last name? It was worth a try. His letter had reached her through Jeremy, Doug, and Katie. That was very resourceful of him.

"Can you help me with the dishes?" Mom asked Sierra just as she was about to flee to the sanctuary of her room.

"Okay," she answered halfheartedly. As she loaded the dishwasher, she considered saying something to Mom about the letter. She almost expected Mom to ask about it. But she didn't, and Sierra decided to keep the secret to herself for a while. Of course she would tell both her mom and dad eventually. But not yet. The secret was too sweet to share with anyone just now. She thought she might even wait a day or two before writing back to Katie.

With an energetic snap of the dial, Sierra turned on the dishwasher and dried her hands.

"You seem to be feeling better," Mom said.

"I guess I am," Sierra said before hurrying up the stairs. She shut her bedroom door and pulled out the letter. She read it one more time. Then two more times. Now she was ready to write back.

But on what? She didn't own any nice paper. Maybe Tawni did. Sierra looked through the desk and didn't find anything she wanted to use.

Then, slipping the letter back under her pillow,

Sierra went down the hall to Granna Mae's room and knocked softly on the door.

"Come in." Granna Mae was watching a rerun of "The Waltons," her favorite TV show.

"I wondered if you had a piece of stationery I could borrow."

Fortunately the commercial came on just then. Granna Mae slowly slid off her bed and shuffled to the old desk in the corner of the room.

"I didn't mean for you to get up," Sierra said. "I could have gotten it."

"No, no, Lovey! I have different stationery for different letters. Is this to a boy or girl?"

"A guy," Sierra said, feeling a little funny admitting it for the first time.

"I have just the thing." Granna Mae pawed through a whole drawer of random single sheets that must have taken her a lifetime to collect. Letterhead stationery from hotels that weren't even in business any longer came out of the desk, as did pink sheets and aqua-colored sheets. Then she pulled out one piece that was the color of wheat. In the bottom right corner in faint calligraphy letters was written "Zephaniah 3:17."

"This is the last of the stationery I used to write to my Paul every day." She handed it to Sierra. "Will this work for you, Lovey?"

The coincidence rattled Sierra a bit. Did Granna Mae somehow know she was writing to a Paul too? "Sure. Yes, thank you. It's perfect. Good night."

She scooted down the hall to her room and closed the door. Sierra stood for a moment with her back against the door, feeling her heart pound.

"You are so real," she breathed into the empty room. "Sometimes, God, You boggle my imagination! Is this a sacred piece of stationery, or what?"

Sierra didn't have to look up the verse at the bottom. She knew it was the one Granna Mae had made her repeat the night she tucked her in, thinking Sierra was Emma. For a flicker of a moment Sierra wondered if maybe Granna Mae wasn't smarter than all of them put together. What if she were only faking this memory lapse thing to make them all move in with her and to give her opportunities to get her points across without being held responsible? No, that couldn't be.

Stretching out on the bed, Sierra held her pen poised over the paper and carefully began to write. She couldn't make any mistakes.

"Paul, Aren't you the clever one, sending messages through your big brother! Big brothers can come in handy sometimes. Like last Friday when my big brother took me to the movies. The funny thing was, I thought I saw someone there who looked just like you. I probably should have said something. One always expects little girls with big mouths to say something, doesn't one?

"Oh, and about your life. It doesn't sound demolished to me. Of course, it's hard to tell yet. You must get a great view up there on that fence. Maybe a few splinters?

"Please tell your mother she's a saint for putting up with your garbage these past—what was it? Ten months? And yes, I do fly. We *did* meet at an airport, didn't we? Sierra."

She carefully addressed the envelope, folded the letter, and placed it inside. Before she sealed it, Sierra had one last thought. Across from the verse she printed her street address in tiny letters the same way Paul had left his box number.

She thought of how much had changed in her life in the past few weeks. She had been to Great Britain and back all by herself; had her faith stretched during the outreach in Northern Ireland; made some wonderful friends; met Paul; settled in a new, old house with a grandmother who was changing right before her eyes; started a new school; and, after letting God break down her stubborn resistance, decided she liked Royal and the people there. Sierra felt as if her emotions and her life were beginning to even out.

Glancing down at the letter one more time, she noticed an open space after her name. She decided to add one final thought that summed up her life right now.

"P.S. By the way, yes, I am happy now. Thanks for asking."

Don't Miss These Captivating Stories in the SIERRA JENSEN SERIES

#1 • Only You, Sierra
During Sierra's weeklong missions trip in Europe, her family moves to a different state. Returning home, she dreads the loneliness of going to a new high school—until she meets Paul in the airport.

#2 • In Your Dreams
Sierra's junior year is nothing like she dreamed. With no job, no friends, a sick grandmother, and a neat-freak sister, her life is becoming a nightmare! And just when things start to go her way—she even gets asked out on a date—Sierra runs into Paul.

#3 • Don't You Wish
Sierra is excited about visiting Christy Miller in California during Easter break. She's ready to relax and leave her troubles behind. Unfortunately, a nagging "trouble" has followed her there—her sister, Tawni! Somehow, Tawni seems to win the attention of everyone . . . even a guy.

#4 • Close Your Eyes
Sparks fly when Sierra runs into Paul while volunteering at a shelter. But the situation gets sticky when Paul comes over for dinner and Randy shows up at the same time.

#5 • Without a Doubt
When Drake—the gorgeous guy Amy likes—reveals his interest in Sierra, life gets complicated. Sierra wonders if she can trust her emotions. And when a freak snowstorm hits during a backpacking trip with her youth group, she is forced to face her doubts.

#6 • With This Ring
Sierra couldn't be happier when she goes to Southern California to join Christy Miller and their friends at the wedding they've all been waiting for. Amid the "I do's" and Tracy and Doug's first kiss ever, Sierra realizes that purity is truly sacred and something worth having.

#7 • Open Your Heart
When Sierra's friend Christy Miller receives a scholarship from a university in Switzerland, she invites Sierra to go with her and Aunt Marti to visit the school. En route there, the two girls meet Alex, a college student from Russia, and Sierra begins looking forward to seeing him again.

The CHRISTY MILLER SERIES

If you've enjoyed reading about Sierra Jensen, you'll love reading about Sierra's friend Christy Miller. She seems like a real-life friend that you can relate to, trust, and get to know.

#1 • Summer Promise
Christy spends the summer at the beach with her wealthy aunt and uncle. Will she do something she'll later regret?

#2 • A Whisper and a Wish
Christy is convinced that dreams do come true when her family moves to California and the cutest guy in school shows an interest in her.

#3 • Yours Forever
Fifteen-year-old Christy does everything in her power to win Todd's attention.

#4 • Surprise Endings
Christy tries out for cheerleader, learns a classmate is out to get her, and schedules two dates for the same night.

#5 • Island Dreamer
It's an incredible tropical adventure when Christy celebrates her sixteenth birthday on Maui.

#6 • A Heart Full of Hope
A dazzling dream date, a wonderful job, a great car. And lots of freedom! Christy has it all. Or docs she?

#7 • True Friends
Christy sets out with the ski club and discovers the group is thinking of doing something more than hitting the slopes.

#8 • Starry Night
Christy is torn between going to the Rose Bowl Parade with her friends or on a surprise vacation with her family.

#9 • Seventeen Wishes
Christy is off to summer camp—as a counselor for a cabin of wild fifth-grade girls.

#10 • A Time to Cherish
A surprise houseboat trip! Her senior year! Lots of friends! Life couldn't be better for Christy until . . .

#11 • Sweet Dreams
Christy's dreams become reality when Todd finally opens his heart to her. But her relationship with her best friend goes downhill fast when Katie starts dating Michael, and Christy has doubts about their relationship.

#12 • A Promise Is Forever
On a European trip with her friends, Christy finds it difficult to keep her mind off Todd. Will God bring them back together?

9802

Young Adult Fiction Series From Bethany House Publishers
(Ages 12 and up)

———❦———

CEDAR RIVER DAYDREAMS • by Judy Baer
Experience the challenges and excitement of high school life with Lexi Leighton and her friends.

GOLDEN FILLY SERIES • by Lauraine Snelling
Tricia Evanston races to become the first female jockey to win the sought-after Triple Crown.

JENNIE MCGRADY MYSTERIES • by Patricia Rushford
A contemporary Nancy Drew, Jennie McGrady's sleuthing talents bring back readers again and again.

LIVE! FROM BRENTWOOD HIGH • by Judy Baer
The staff of an action-packed teen-run news show explores the love, laughter, and tears of high school life.

THE SPECTRUM CHRONICLES • by Thomas Locke
Adventure awaits readers in this fantasy series set in another place and time.

SPRINGSONG BOOKS • by various authors
Compelling love stories and contemporary themes promise to capture the hearts of readers.

WHITE DOVE ROMANCES • by Yvonne Lehman
Romance, suspense, and fast-paced action for teens committed to finding pure love.